THE ACADEMY

◆ ◆ ◆

The Academy
Orientation
Book 1

◆ ◆ ◆

CHAPTER ONE

◆ ◆ ◆

Nestled high on a hill in the quaint picturesque town of Kentville, Connecticut is where you will find The Academy. A privately owned boarding college quietly tucked away in the area of the state called the Litchfield Hills. The land is vast and filled with the scenic beauty that New England is known for. It's bountiful with breathtaking views of lakes, parks, forests, and natural waterfalls in addition to classic farm houses and eye catching architecture.

The Academy is a prestigious and highly respected college that caters to some of the most gifted & intelligent student athletes there are. On the grounds you'll find walking & running trails, fields, lakes, an outdoor pool with sundeck, and several buildings that are all part of the campus. The main building contains all of the classrooms, as well as, offices for the teachers. A little way across the beautiful lawn from the main building is the recreation center complete with an internet cafe, a movie theater, a fully equipped gym, weight room, and yoga room. There is also an indoor pool and Jacuzzi that is extremely popular in the winter months.

Adjacent to the main building but slightly set back further across the lawn is the a building labeled Discipline Hall. This is the one building that students don't want to find themselves in. It serves a very useful and special purpose in correcting bad behavior and handling wayward students.

The boys and girls dorms at The Academy are spectacular. They are all large, beautifully furnished with1 bedroom in a condo style layout. Each student has their own room and it is a requirement that all students attending the school reside here in these dorms.

The Academy maintains a low profile in the hills of Connecticut but those that do know about it are very familiar with it's history. It is consistently ranked among the top 20 boarding schools in the country. It's one of the most desired private schools for athletically gifted & equally intelligent students seeking a 4 year degree. Getting into the school is almost impossible since it's student base never exceeds 40 students per year and the screening process is very selective. The school is co-ed and strives to maintain a fairly even ratio of boys to girls.

It was founded by Marilyn and Marjorie Devlin. Two sisters that also own farms connected to the property. Each & every student that attends the school must work at various jobs on the property. These jobs include everything from grounds & pool maintenance, to office work and cleaning. Other jobs can include teaching yoga classes, fitness training, and tutoring. Some students even work at the farms owned by Ms. Marilyn and Ms. Marj.

The school continues to operate pretty much the same as it did since it's inception. It focuses on strict old fashion values with a no nonsense, zero tolerance policy for misbehavior. Minimum age to attend the college is 18. Due to it's prestige and uniqueness the tuition is very expensive. Gaining a scholarship to this school is extremely rare and many wealthy parents are ecstatic to have their kids accepted to The Academy right after high school graduation. The school has a successful track record of it's graduates that speaks for itself. It's known for producing some of the most intelligent and respected sport doctors, naturopathic doctors, coaches, and trainers in the country. In addition, it has spawned some amazing professional athletes, fitness models, & even Olympians.

Being a physically gifted athlete isn't the only requirement to get into this school. You also have to be nothing short of brilliant. Everything from the entrance exam right down to the curriculum & physical training is something that is incredibly demanding. Since there is a maximum of 40 students attending the school during a semester it ensures an excellent teacher to student ratio. This coupled with a dedicated faculty that really nurtures students, is the main reason for it's success and it's reputation. The school consists of an all female staff made up of Principal Katherine "Kate" Kensington, teachers Jennifer Summers, Brooke Colston, Paige Daniels, Carrie Ann Morena, and the school Nurse Madison Sinclair. All faculty is respectfully called by their first name preceded with Ms. This has been established by Ms. Marilyn who felt using first names made it less formal but yet still respectful.

As co-founders, Ms. Marilyn and Ms. Marj still oversee many things and attend every Monday morning staff meeting. However, it is clear that Principal Kate is truly the one in charge day to day. Ms. Marilyn used to be the school principal since it's inception but 4 years ago she and her sister Marj had the opportunity to really expand the farm. They found themselves traveling more as the demand for their farm products were highly sought after. Around this same time Marilyn decided to purchase a second home in Naples, Florida to escape the cold New England winter. It wasn't long after that Marjorie did the same. Now both sisters spend their winter months in the warm climate of Florida. During these winter months they make it a point to still participate in every Monday morning staff meeting thru video calling.

Ms. Marilyn is a vibrant, healthy woman who defies her age of 56. She has reddish brown hair styled just below her shoulders. She keeps herself in great shape and she is quite attractive. Ms. Marj is 54, looks similar and is also energetic and physically fit.

Since it is a private college and they call the shots, the teachers they hire are all physical fit as well. They have very old fashion values and truly believe in the saying "lead by example". Both sisters are ecstatic at the way Principal Kate runs the school. She is totally dedicated and her no nonsense philosophy is a perfect match to everything the two sisters believe in. They love how she maintains the same old fashion values they've established years ago. The Academy has and always will operate on these values with zero tolerance for misbehaving students.

All students have to be at least 18 years old to attend the school. They are required to read and sign the school handbook, as well as, the

education contract, & consent form before enrollment. All parents and guardians must read and
sign as well, even though at age 18 in Connecticut you are considered a legal adult. All the rules
and school guidelines are explained in detail in
this student handbook. It clearly states that any
teacher or faculty member has the authority to
use corporal punishment to discipline a student
for infractions and misbehavior. This means anything such as poor grades, skipping school, work
infractions, rudeness, disrespect, breaking curfew,
drinking and missing workouts to name a few.
With a zero tolerance policy any student caught
with narcotics, performance enhancing drugs,
steroids, or convicted of a crime will be automat-
ically expelled and the tuition paid is forfeited.

The students totally understand the strict
guidelines of the school. They constantly praise
and respect the faculty for being loving & nurturing women that really care about them. However,
they also understand these women all have a very
stern side that falls in line with the school's no
nonsense approach.

Each teacher along with the school nurse
has been properly trained in the various methods
of handling & disciplining students. Every student
knows that each of these loving but stern women
have been given the reform school strap and the
official school wooden paddle to use on them.
They also understand that the faculty has the

freedom to use any other implement or means of punishment they see fit, it states that very clearly in the student handbook and consent form. It also states they will be suspended or even permanently kicked out of the school for serious offenses. These have been the rules and method of operation that Ms. Marilyn and Ms. Marj created upon the schools inception. At first they were hesitant when they pondered stepping down from the day to day management of the school. This was especially a tough decision for Ms. Marilyn who took on most of the administrative burden as school Principal.

How can the school manage to run efficiently with us away for the winter?

How can it maintain its old fashion values and prestigious status?

Well that was all put to rest after Katherine Kensington interviewed for the position of School Principal 4 years ago.

CHAPTER TWO

◆ ◆ ◆

K ate Kensington had just turned 31 years old when she interviewed for the highly respected and demanding position of principal. Her credentials were excellent as a graduate with a degree in Psychology. She had several years of employment as a guidance counselor for a private catholic high school and within 3 years, was then promoted to the assistant principal of that school. Her resume looked great but her interview with Ms. Marilyn is what really mattered and sealed the deal. Kate walked into the interview having the professionalism and confidence that had to be witnessed to be believed. She was dressed in a classic business suit with her shoulder length blonde hair styled perfectly. Her big green eyes and curvy athletic figure spoke volumes before any words came out of her mouth.

Then once she did speak Ms. Marilyn was simply floored!

Her interview lasted over 2 hours and she absolutely impressed Ms. Marilyn. To have this much professional experience and to have been the assistant principal of the catholic high school at age 31, definitely commanded attention.

Ms. Marilyn was also impressed and surprised to learn that Kate had a very successful career in competitive mixed martial arts. Kate explained that she was no longer competing but still practiced and currently held a 4th degree black belt in Tae Kwan Do.

All of this was further confirmation for Ms. Marilyn that Kate would be the perfect principal to run her school. She totally understood commitment, training, & most of all discipline. During the interview Kate explained her life in detail. It felt more like a nice comfortable conversation than an interview. Kate was totally relaxed in this environment with Ms. Marilyn and she went on to thoroughly explain how she came from a very strict upbringing. This is where Ms. Marilyn really took in all that Kate was saying. She went on to explain how she was raised in a strict catholic family with a loving but stern Mom and Dad. She was the middle child and along with her 2 other sisters grew up in a house with a zero tolerance policy for misbehaving. So the zero tolerance policy that The Academy student handbook detailed, is something Kate had already lived and experienced in her own life.

Kate explained when her dad passed away how her mom had to raise the 3 teenage girls alone. She made this reference and gave credit to how those teenage years really molded her into the woman she was today. She went on to say how this was so similar to the methods of discipline described in The Academy's student handbook. She described to Ms. Marilyn the details of how she and her sisters were often on the receiving end of bare bottom spankings. In addition to using her hand, her mom might also use the wooden spoon, or strap if she felt it necessary. Ms. Marilyn smirked and even smiled on the inside hearing this.

She proceeded to ask Kate even more questions and listened more intently. "Since you have been spanked as a teenager it seems that you are very familiar with this style of discipline to handle misbehaving boys and girls. Is that correct Kate?" Ms. Marilyn asked.

Kate without hesitation responded with a confidence Ms. Marilyn hadn't seen in previous interviews. "Oh God yes ma' am, on both sides... getting and giving."

"I'm no stranger to spankings. You see not

only did I get them growing up but I also gave my share of spankings when I attended college and worked for a wealthy family as their live-in nanny."

She went on to explain that during her college years she attended a school in Texas that was similar to The Academy. She told Ms. Marilyn that her mom was instrumental and highly recommended this school since it was a small and privately run college. She joked that her Mom was suddenly on board and pushed for her to attend this school once she knew it used spankings and corporal punishment as a disciplinary method.

Kate further went on to explain that the only difference was that students could reside off campus. She then gave Ms. Marilyn all the details on how she got a job as the live-in nanny for 2 teenagers, a girl age 17 and a boy 16. It was the perfect job since both of their parents worked nights as full time musicians. Sometimes they had gigs on Wednesday nights but they were always totally booked from Thursdays thru Sundays. They were very in demand, made a lot of money, and many times worked double shifts on Saturdays and Sundays playing weddings and parties in addition to night clubs.

This job allowed Kate to go to school during the day where she took as many classes on Mondays, Tuesdays, and Wednesdays as possible.

This still allowed her some free time to exercise and study on those nights and it was a perfect match, plus she was compensated well and didn't have the extra expense of living on campus.

"When I started as their nanny they were just completely disobedient and disrespectful. They basically acted like spoiled brats and had average grades in school." Kate told her.

"I explained to their parents how I was spanked as a teenager and how I would handle their kids the exact same way. I would be just as caring and loving as my parents but also stern when I needed to be. Their parents never spanked them and they were very lackadaisical in their approach, lacking structure or any type of punishment. Most of the times they would just take away their video games or try the reward system."

"Well, that simply didn't work for them." Kate went on and further impressed her.

"I did my research and shared many books, articles, and facts with them on the positive effects from spanking. How it was more common in America years ago and behavior was much better. The best results actually occurred when spankings were administered by non-parents. So any authoritative figures like teachers, principals, governesses, headmasters, law enforcement, even babysitters made a huge difference. The research documented that the combination of being exposed, embarrassed, vulnerable and account-able to someone other than a parent as the reasons for producing these outstanding results."

"Then I shared the facts about how it's still prominently used in other countries." Kate further explained.

Kate knew her stuff and Ms. Marilyn was totally engaged and blown away by her knowledge. She wanted to hear more. She wanted to hear every detail from Kate.

"So tell me more Kate. Those books and articles is that what convinced them?"

"Well, I reminded them that Texas is a pro-spanking state and corporal punishment is a very common method of discipline for families and even in public schools there. They agreed and gave me the authority to spank."

"I assured them it was an extension of love. I would always fully discuss the reasons to spank and afterwards I would still be a caring and nurturing role model to them." Kate stated very clearly.

She went on to give Ms. Marilyn the many details of the way she handled these 2 unruly teens. She shared the various spanking positions & implements that she used. She spoke of the way she would have to hold them in place if they were kicking and squirming when she spanked them. It was clear to Ms. Marilyn that Kate knew a lot about spanking and that she absolutely had the experience. Kate mentioned how it wasn't long before the parents witnessed a complete 360 change with the behavior of their two teenagers. She further explained how the wealthy couple kept her employed for her entire college years in Texas. She was proud to state how quickly they became straight A students. Even more importantly, is how they learned a level of respect that they still carry with them today.

Kate added, "Guess what happened? There were many times over the years that these kids would actually come to me and ask me to spank them and ground them."

She saw how Ms. Marilyn's eye brows suddenly raised up higher. She went on to further explain how they really started respecting themselves and had enough internal discipline to know when they were starting to slack off. Ms. Marilyn now totally enthralled, took in every word as Kate shared how they went on to apply themselves as much as they could in school and once they started getting excellent grades they became even more committed. She stressed how it became a priority for them to maintain these grades.

"There were many times they felt they needed to study more and avoid distractions, goofing around, and going out with their friends. This is when they would simply come to me and ask for a spanking and to also ground them. This forced them to stay home and study more." Kate relayed as Ms. Marilyn nodded her head in a yes motion.

"They actually coined the phrase a PM spanking. They would come to me and say Kate, I have a huge test and I really need to study. If you ground me I will have an excuse not to go out when my friends call. Plus, if you give me a spanking for preventative maintenance I would be reminded of it when I sit down and study. It would really help me focus." She relayed to Ms. Marilyn with a slight giggle.

"WOW! They really understood the consequences of their actions, as well as, holding themselves accountable." Ms. Marilyn replied. "I like that. The kids learned enough respect for their own behavior to ask you to spank them. Outstanding Kate!"

"Yes ma'am" Kate replied. "Like I said, I'm no stranger to yanking pants down and putting a shade of red on a bare hiney. I'm a stern no nonsense spanker just like my mom. I've used everything from my hand, to paddle, to wooden spoon. However, I must tell you that my favorite implement to use is a strap. It always works wonders. So I'm very familiar with using an old fashion reform school type strap like the one you mention in your handbook."

Ms. Marilyn now in complete awe of Kate's confidence replied "I'm actually impressed that you used the word hiney and you didn't swear or use the word ass. We try our best not to swear around here. We make it an effort to use old fashion alternate words like hiney, fanny, bottom, butt, rear end, instead." Ms. Marilyn explained.

"Well ma'am, swearing was not allowed at all in my house growing up. If my mom heard a swear someone was getting spanked. Plus, if it was a really bad word we might get our mouth washed out with soap." Kate replied.

"Hmmm, I see." Ms. Marilyn replied.

"Yep, the struggle was real." Kate immediately made Ms. Marilyn laugh out loud.

"Plus, now I'm a single mom to a 6 year old son, Joshua. His dad and I have been divorced for 4 years and I do everything I can to avoid swearing around him. I'm pretty stern with him and thankfully I have my mom as a staple in his life too. She is a great help babysitting and picking him up from school. My son already understands the importance of good behavior because he has 2 strict Kensington women watching him." Kate further mentioned.

Ms. Marilyn then asked "So Kate it's obvious that you are in amazing physical shape. The students here at this school are physically strong. Mostly they will co-operate because they all signed the consent form. If they don't accept their punishment their enrollment will be terminated. It's understood they have a choice and it's their decision. However, even though this is the case, I have given quite a few spankings where they squirm, try to block or twist away. It's just a natural reaction. How will you handle that?"

"I use my voice to sternly scold and warn them as a first step. That is usually all it takes for them to realize it can get worse if they don't listen. If not then I also have a vast knowledge of various holds. I'm convinced that my martial arts training helps as well. I've also used about every spanking position there is. Trust me ma'am, I'm not one to be underestimated in the strength department either." Kate answered with complete confidence.

Ms. Marilyn suddenly had the idea that not only would she hire Kate as principal but she would also start a mandatory discipline training program for all the female teachers. Refresher type sessions every 6 months to review spanking techniques, share new ideas, holds, implements, etc. Kate would be perfect to lead these sessions and provide the existing teachers with even more knowledge regarding spankings. So just as quick as Kate walked into the interview she walked out with her new position as principal of The Acad-emy.

CHAPTER THREE

◆ ◆ ◆

During the years that Kate took over, the school continued to operate more efficiently than ever. To this day, The Academy has been prominently featured in various magazines and publications. It is now nationally recognized as one of the top five 4 year boarding colleges in America.

Ms. Marilyn is more than proud but always tries to avoid over exposure as she likes having her school a bit under the radar and hidden in the quaint Connecticut countryside. She has been beyond pleased with the performance of Principal Kate both from the nurturing side and the no nonsense stern side. Plus, she witnesses first hand how physically active Kate is.

You can often find the attractive principal

in the school gym working out early in the morning before work. Sometimes you will find her teaming up with her peer Ms. Jenn at lunch or even after school for a workout as well. Kate is always quick to help students that ask her advice on specific exercises, nutrition, and even the way she demonstrates her technique for hitting and kicking the punching bags. At times she may even take a student thru a workout with her. It's clear everyone really likes and respects her as principal.

This respect for her is even more prominent when it comes time for her to be stern and carry out discipline. Both Ms. Marilyn and Ms. Marj who never hesitated to spank and discipline a student now often find themselves sending naughty boys and girls directly to Principal Kate's office. Many times these students are then marched straight to Discipline Hall where the strict principal is quick to deal with them.

Ms. Marilyn makes it a point to often compliment Kate for the way she is running the school. She is especially impressed with the way she handles misbehaving students. It wasn't long ago that Ms. Marilyn got a ring side seat and actually witnessed the strong principal deliver quite a spanking. Needless to say, she was even more impressed and satisfied. She was quite proud and glowing from her decision to hire Kate as principal.

It happened one day when Kate was over at Ms. Marilyn's farm house. The two of them were having coffee and discussing school business in her kitchen, when she noticed 2 students Julia and Cassie having a huge disagreement outside on the farm. It was escalating and almost at the verge of getting physical. Julia was pretty heated and really yelling at Cassie. Kate took a moment while talking to Ms. Marilyn to stand up and glance out the open window. She then put her ear to the screen and listened closely to the ruckus and commotion going on outside. She observed Julia, a very cute, petite, athletic first year student with an amazingly strong looking physique and unfortunately for her, a mouth that seemed just as strong.

Julia was now yelling, overheated, and really getting out of hand. She was having more than just words with Cassie, a taller stunning brunette that was in her 2nd year at the school. It seemed Julia didn't like taking orders from another student even though Cassie had the position of delegating farm chores.

One thing led to another and before you know it Julia was in Cassie's face arguing about her farm chores. Things started to really elevate as Julia began swearing and throwing F-bombs at Cassie. Cassie showed much reserve and stayed cool knowing what could happen if she retaliated.

23

When her words crossed into the physical level is when Principal Kate stepped in with a purpose. Cassie was marched into Discipline Hall and giving a spanking that she will never forget. The images of Principal Kate stripping her down to her birthday suit and applying the reform strap to her bare bottom was still prominent in Cassie's mind. She was well aware of what could happen if she got physical with Julia. So instead, she backed off and stayed cool as Julia continued yelling and swearing at her. Before things got any more intense Kate turned to Ms. Marilyn and said, "Excuse me for a moment please."

Within seconds Kate jogged hastily over to the 2 girls and yelled.

"Hey, knock it off you two!"

She approached as Julia was yelling and swearing up a storm with "fuck this" and "fuck that". Then she actually pushed Cassie and gave her the finger. This is when Principal Kate really sprung into action. She grabbed Julia with one hand on her earlobe and the other with a firm grip of her upper arm. The petite student immediately let out a loud "Oooow" from the force of Kate's grip.

"Julia you are going to be one sorry young lady. MARCH Missy.. MOVE IT!" Kate scolded in a stern tone while marching Julia back in the direction of Ms. Marilyn's house.

Ms. Marilyn watched as her stern, young principal was forcefully escorting Julia back towards her home. Julia did all she could and tried her best to apologize and plead but Principal Kate simply wasn't having it. Ms. Marilyn now held the door open and watched Kate drag Julia right into her large living room. She didn't interrupt and just observed as Kate backed Julia into a corner of the room scolding her the entire time. She reminded Julia about signing her consent form and if she wanted out. Julia still overheated remained silent and just shook her head with a no direction.

Now standing face to face with the irate student, Kate aggressively reached down and gave one swift tug on Julia's cute nylon exercise shorts completely exposing her. Julia was stunned and embarrassed as she naturally moved her arms and quickly tried to cover her vagina with her hands.

"Oh you can try to cover up all you want. I've seen it all before young lady." Kate scolded sternly.

She then forcefully grabbed Julia's left arm and spun her around face into the corner with her bare hiney out. Not letting go, she quickly raised Julia's left arm holding it tight and high over her head. Then in a split second, Kate maneuvered and moved her own left arm underneath Julia's and around the back of her neck.

It resembled some type of half nelson wrestling or martial arts hold. Julia still stunned attempted to squirm, and twist but Kate held her firmly with the hold. She then raised her right arm back and delivered a flurry of intense hand slaps across Julia's bare bottom instantly making her dance from leg to leg.

"<SLAP>, Don't you ever <SLAP, SLAP>… Ever.. <SLAP>… Let me see you being aggressive <SLAP>… or causing trouble <SLAP>… or swearing like that in this school again. <SLAP, SLAP, SLAP>…. Is that clear MISSY!" The strict principal sternly scolded as her strong right hand was reddening Julia's behind. The moment Julia felt the sting of Kate's intense first slap she immediately let out a tone that confirmed the sting she felt. Then as Kate landed each additional slap on her bare bottom she couldn't hold it in any longer and the tears formed in her eyes.

Ms. Marilyn watched in awe of how quickly Kate took control of Julia and how she held her in place despite Julia's natural reaction of trying to wiggle and squirm away during the spanking. On that day her eyes witnessed first hand how capable Principal Kate was in delivering a spanking and handling a situation like this.

Kate continued to spank with her strong hand making Julia dance in place as some tears now rolled down her face. "Get that fanny out

Julia! <SLAP>... Stick it out farther... <SLAP, SLAP>" Kate would further scold each time her hand connected to Julia's rear end. As a natural reaction, Julia would clench her cheeks and tuck her body inward toward the wall from the hard stinging slaps Kate was delivering. "I said stick that fanny out young lady! <SLAP, SLAP>." Kate sternly reiterated.

Ms. Marilyn watched intently as Kate delivered these potent slaps to the once feisty, and aggressive student. Kate then reached down and pulled Julia shorts from around her knees and slid them all the way down to her ankles. She eyed her butt and made sure that every inch of it was properly displaying evidence of her firm hand print.

<SLAP, SLAP>... continued to echo off the living rooms walls of Ms. Marilyn's home in stereo with the "OOOww" from Julia's voice.

Julia tried but couldn't stand still as her natural reaction of wiggling and tucking her hips inward was still happening despite Principal Kate's scolding to keep her hiney out. Kate realized this was a natural reaction to the pain she felt from those hard stinging slaps. This is when Principal Kate decided to change her hold in order to keep Julia's fanny out further for the remainder of her spanking. Principal Kate then quickly placed her left arm around and under Julia's waist. With one fluid motion Kate shifted her weight and then yanked Julia over her curvy left hip. This made Julia's rear end stick out exactly where the stern Principal wanted it to be. Her eyes were now even more glued on Julia's cute bare bottom.

Ms. Marilyn was witnessing first hand just how experienced her young principal was at giving a spanking. As a principal, Ms. Marilyn always had the reputation of being a hard spanker. However, her style was much more old fashion and traditional. She would either bend students over the desk, make them lie flat on their stomach, or take them over her knee. She never used or had ever seen the type of holds that Kate was using on Julia.

Now that Principal Kate held Julia firmly in place over her hip, she raised her right arm back again and with eyes focused like a laser on her target the strong principal delivered one last flurry of hand slaps to Julia's rear end. Kate landed at least 6, 7 maybe even 10 in row across Julia's perfectly round butt and even extended a few down to the top of her legs.

Julia was now dancing over Kate's hip but to no avail as Kate maintained a strong hold on her. Even with her squirming, twisting, and kicking Kate's grip kept her secure and right where she wanted her. Principal Kate delivered one of her no nonsense spankings that the newly enrolled student would always remember. Julia's cheeks were completely red without any white showing thanks to Kate's strong hand. She then released Julia and spun her around telling her to stand face in the corner with her fanny out. Julia did exactly what Kate said without wasting a second.

Kate then turned to Ms. Marilyn with a cute smirk and said, "Now where were we?"

CHAPTER FOUR

◆ ◆ ◆

Th
he two women walked back into the kitchen and continued to talk school business as Julia's bright red hiney remained
on display in the living room. When Kate and Ms.
Marilyn finished their discussion of school business, the principal called out the door to Cassie to
come inside the house. The 2nd year student came
in with a scared look in her eyes. She was so petri-
fied that Principal Kate was going to spank her
that she already had tears forming. Principal Kate
walked Cassie into the living room and showed
her Julia, standing in the corner with a bare, bright
red, hand printed bottom on display. Cassie's
mouth just opened as her eyes took in the sight.
Julia's head turned over her shoulder as she looked
at Cassie. Still sobbing Julia wasted no time and
without even a cue from Principal Kate she said,

"I'm sorry Cass… I was way out of line and wrong."

Ms. Marilyn still taking all this in was amazed at the result and how quickly Julia apologized. Cassie accepted her apology and Principal Kate excused both students to resume their work. There would be no doubt that everyone working on the farm would see evidence of what just happened to Julia as the top of her legs showed deep red hand prints that her exercise shorts couldn't hide. Before she walked out the door Julia turned to Principal Kate and also apologized with tears still in her eyes. Principal Kate immediately displayed her nurturing side and gave Julia a warm, loving hug.

Then she wiped the tears from her face and softly said, "I accept your apology sweetie. I know you're feisty but be careful not to let it get the best of you. Do whatever you can not to get overheated like that again. Agreed?"

Julia shook her head in a yes motion. Kate then asked her, "How much longer are you working?" Julia looked at the clock in Ms. Marilyn's kitchen. It was 4:30pm. She replied, "until 5 Ma'am."

"Okay hold on, let me call Nurse Madison." Kate picked up her cell phone and talked.

"Hi Maddy, can you stay a little after 5? I'm sending Julia to you. She will be needing some ointment and some lotion applied to her rear end and the top of her legs."

Nurse Madison must have made a joke because Kate's reply was all that Julia and Ms. Marilyn heard. She said as she smirked and looked at Julia, "Well, let's just say that my hand and her hiney really got to know each other."

"OK, thank you Maddy. I promise it shouldn't take long and won't interfere with you going to yoga class." Kate ensured.

Kate then instructed Julia to go straight to Nurse Madison right after work. Once again the young student shook her head in a yes motion and walked out of the house. It was in that moment on that day when Ms. Marilyn witnessed first hand the stern side, as well as, the loving side of her new principal. Kate was the person she knew could handle this school as good, if not better, than she even did.

Ever since Kate was hired as principal it seems every teacher has also stepped up their game regarding spankings and discipline. To this day Monday classes don't start until 1pm because the women of The Academy conduct their weekly staff meeting at 9am followed by lunch. Everything from school budget to activities are discussed, even exercise and social events between the staff are shared.

Each teacher takes the time to talk about their past week, as well as, their upcoming plans for the week ahead. All disciplining sessions are fully discussed in detail as well. The teachers review their log reports stating the students name, the type of infraction, and the method of discipline. Every detail is discussed right down to the positions and implements that the teacher used. They classify spankings on levels usually ranging from 5-10.

Level 5 is basically the maintenance type of spanking that Principal Kate has put in effect since she started. Even though a level 5 spanking is restricted to just being a hand spanking, it is still very effective and of course it still hurts and gives quite a sting. It's enough to make an impression and correct behavior. Most students may still tear up a bit and can usually feel the after effects the next day.

A level 10 spanking would be considered the hardest, usually using the reform strap and/or wooden paddle. Most discipline spankings that teachers and Principal Kate give fall around a level 7-8. The women actually find it helpful to review these log reports at the Monday morning meetings. They don't hesitate to discuss and share tips on what worked and what didn't when handling misbehavior. Nurse Madison also discusses in detail her review of students physical examinations, vitamins & supplements, and any illnesses or potential threats that may be going around campus.

Ms. Marilyn has been so impressed with Principal Kate that she has put in the mandatory discipline training session for the faculty. These sessions happen about every 6 months and Kate takes the lead teaching and demonstrating for Ms. Jenn, Ms. Brooke, Ms. Paige, Ms. Carrie Ann, Ms. Marj and Ms. Marilyn. The teachers then partner up and try these various techniques, implements, and holds.

Since this is a hands on training session teachers have to practice giving and then also being on the receiving end of these spankings during this training. So needless to say, about every six months the women faculty get a fresh reminder on what a good bare bottom spanking still feels like.

CHAPTER FIVE

❖ ❖ ❖

T o this day all students must live on the campus and must work at various jobs at the school. A select few students may also reside with Ms. Marilyn or Ms. Marj during the semester. This is considered a very prestigious honor since these students really get a one-on-one loving relationship with the founders. This is very similar to the old-fashion boarding school that both Ms. Marilyn and Ms. Marj attended when they were students. The "boarding" students living with Ms. Marj & Ms. Marilyn usually refer to them as their "Dorm-Mom or Boarding Teacher" showing a high level respect for these 2 women.

A new semester is about to begin at The Academy and several new students arrive. Among the select few is Jordan Thompson. Jordan is one of these gifted athletic and super intelligent students. He is a straight "A" student out of a catholic high school and his interests are in naturopathic medicine and fitness modeling. He is extremely focused, works hard on his physique, and does his school work with the same intensity.

Jordan has those natural good looks with his spiky, dirty blonde "surfer hair" and big green eyes. He has a beautiful physique that is muscular and sexy without being too freakishly over developed, sporting nice wide shoulders that taper into a small defined six pack waist and leading out to muscular legs. To say he has no problem getting dates would be an understatement. Girls swoon over him.

Classes are set to begin next week as this week is dedicated to student orientation and having them settle into their amazing dorms. Jordan has spent the last several days meeting with and talking to each teacher in detail. So far he has really enjoyed the orientation process and the time that each teacher gave to him. He felt very welcomed here at The Academy and couldn't help but notice how attractive all of his teachers are.

He loved the conversations with Ms. Brooke and Ms. Paige. They both had a cool, laid-back vibe about them that instantly made him relax. His orientation with Ms. Carrie Ann touched on everything from world travel, to spinning and cross-fit classes that she loves taking. He was quick to notice her voluptuous physique and olive toned skin. She was very attractive, exotic looking and very personable. They had an easy flowing conversation that easily could have went on and on. Jordan also spent time on the farms of both co-founders Ms. Marilyn and Ms. Marj. He spent an entire day divided evenly with each of them. He was excited to tour their old farmhouses and he enjoyed talking to some of the students that were about to intern and reside there.

His conversations with Ms. Marilyn and Ms. Marj covered everything from school, to animals, to agriculture, to architecture, and even outside interests and current events. He really connected with them, as well as, their dogs. Time flew by that day and he didn't want to leave especially after falling in love and playing catch with his new four legged buddies.

Jordan's orientation with Ms. Jenn was pure fun. Aside from her being incredibly attractive she was totally cool and one of the best things is that she loved football. They talked in so much detail about their favorite teams, the new NFL rules, free agency, etc. He was blown away by how much she really loved it. She also talked proudly of her 3 kids, 2 boys, and 1 girl. Of course her boys were already playing football in school and her daughter was already on the cheerleading team. He also noticed that she had a real warm and nurturing side. It just came natural to her and it was part of her aura. She must be a very cool and understanding mom he thought. So Jordan summed up his orientation with Ms. Jenn as the hot, cool, football mom.

One thing that's clear to Jordan is how the staff really takes their time getting to know each and every student. The only slight disappointment during orientation week was that he didn't get to sit and talk to Nurse Madison. He really loves the medical field and was looking forward to picking her brain and hearing her experience.

Unfortunately, his time with her was very brief due to her hectic schedule. To say that she was busy that day would be an understatement, she was flat out bonkers by all of the paperwork on her desk. She was on the phone scheduling all the students for their physicals while entering data on the computer and updating their medical records. She apologized for having to postpone his orientation with her and mentioned how this time of year is complete madness for her.

She stood up and while extending to shake his hand said, "Don't worry honey, I'll be contacting you in the next month or so once I get caught up with this paperwork."

"No problem, I understand Ma'am." he stated with respect.

He couldn't help but noticed how pretty she was and how toned her arms were. His eyes held a slightly longer than normal stare at her thin, long, pretty fingers as she extended her hand and shook his.

She then gave him a cute smirk and quickly looked him up and down. With a slight twinkle in her eye she said, "I promise you sweetie, we will have plenty of time to talk. Your orientation with me will be just as thorough as your school physical."

Of course Jordan's mind wandered with countless thoughts of the pretty nurse but he managed to stay composed. He was a bit disappointed to leave her so soon but exited her office with anticipation for his physical.

CHAPTER SIX

◆ ◆ ◆

Jordan is now onto his last orientation meeting of the week. He is on route to Principal Kate's office to meet her. Every new student gets to meet with and talk to Principal Kate in her office and then she proceeds to take them on a full walking tour of the campus. He knocks on her door and then enters after he hears a sweet voice say, "come right in". He immediately feels weak in the knees and is completely caught off guard by her beauty.

The pretty principal stands up from behind her desk and extends her hand introducing herself and motioning for him to sit. As they start to talk Jordan's eyes wander around her office, and he begins to take in the pictures of her with MMA greats, professional athletes, and famous coaches. There she is in a photo with Ronda Rousey. Then another with Floyd Mayweather and another with some karate coaches.

He also looks at her trophies and medals and thinks to himself not only is she freakin' hot but she is a total bad ass! Principal Kate greeted Jordan with the same nurturing mannerism that she greats all first time students. She only talks briefly and instead listens intently about their interests, goals, and life plans. The students talk about their childhood, their upbringing, past schools, as well as, any other topics they want to discuss. Nothing is off limits, they can even discuss sex. The faculty in no way outwardly promotes students having sex, however, it knows students will be having it, so they constantly educate. They do all they can to make sure it's always consensual, safe, and not in public.

Usually, this is Nurse Madison's area and she handles the majority of these type of questions and topics. She's in charge of physical exams, monitoring birth control, and will even provide condoms or other methods of protection to keep students educated and aware of the importance of safe sex. Since some students connect better with different teachers, any of them are always available and there to listen and offer advice on this subject. They all ensure total confidentiality unless a crime or a major infraction happens.

Kate was aware that Jordan didn't have his

orientation meeting with Nurse Madison due to her hectic schedule, so she gave Jordan the "low down" in her own "no nonsense way" about the school policy on sex. It was quick and straight to the point.

"OK, let's talk about sex. Don't do it in public we have camera's everywhere. Make sure it's consensual. Always use condoms because an unexpected pregnancy or sexual disease can really kill the vibe and change your life. I have condoms here in my office, so if you need them just ask. Oh and did I mention there are camera's everywhere? So don't do it anywhere in public on campus." She said again, as they both laughed.

She then proceeded to respond to a number of questions from the handsome new student. He seems especially interested in her martial arts background and her physical training. Kate also finds herself drawn into Jordan and the way he carries himself. He seems so much more mature and is definitely more focused then many of the first year students, she thought to herself.

Throughout their in depth conversation they cover a variety of topics without effort. They easily discuss school, work, exercise, goals, and career choices. They even talked about relationships and the importance of balancing everything. She was super impressed when their conversation openly discussed sickness and family health issues that have touched both of their lives.

Usually students are more reserved even intimidated upon meeting their new school principal for the first time. Not Jordan, he was able to hold an intelligent conversation with openness and confidence. He was completely present in the moment and genuinely interested in hearing her life experience and how she got to where she is today.

Principal Kate takes notice of this and makes sure to compliment him. She tells him that aside from being very intelligent, he also has what she calls street smarts and great common sense. She explains that sometimes brilliant people are just book smart but they lack common sense. She also can't help but take notice of his amazing physique and how naturally good looking he is. They continued to have an effortless conversation discussing everything under the sun. She thinks to herself, damn I wish he was older. I connect more with him than I do with guys my age.

For some reason her mind starts having some unexpected thoughts about him. Since her divorce and in her 4 years with the school, she never felt a connection or these type of feelings for anyone else let alone a student. Lost, daydreaming for a moment, she manages to bring her attention back to the present conversation and finishes answering all of his questions.

She then suggests they walk and tour the campus grounds. During their walk she explains more rules of the school in detail. As they walk across the lawn she first takes him into the building labeled Recreation Center. She explains that this building has the gym, weight room, lockers, and indoor pool. She informs him that it's open 24/7 with his student code but absolutely no outside visitors are allowed before 9am and after 6pm. She also mentions again that there are hidden security cameras everywhere.

During the tour she pauses and lets Jordan go ahead of her exploring the different weight machines. Her eyes seem to be constantly locked on his physique, especially his cute, tight ass in those jeans. More thoughts and images start to enter her mind. She also pictures herself yanking his pants down and spanking that amazing ass.

She loves having that authority and power. It's a huge part of her and she actually gets off on it. So needless to say, there's no way these thoughts are letting up. Kate is well aware what's happening. She's infatuated, maybe smitten but also remains very professional as she continues the tour.

She then shows him the movie theater, game room, cafe, and continues to walk to the outdoor pool. She explains how every student will serve various jobs at the school. The two of them continue their walk having great conversation about weight training, nutrition, and their favorite professional sports and teams. After touring and showing him the Recreation Center they continue across the vast lawn.

She now begins to tell him about the final building, Discipline Hall. They walk directly toward it and Kate says in a semi stern voice. "This is the building I will take you to if you misbehave my dear." They now enter the building and Kate locks the door. She walks Jordan around and points out that there are several different rooms. Each room in Discipline Hall contains a small amount of furniture. One room has a padded upside down U shaped bench. Kate mentions this is used for the straddle type or bent over spanking position. Another room has a padded type massage table and a few other pieces.

They take a quick glance through the open door. Jordan says nothing but just takes it all in unphased. They now enter the biggest room which is considered the main room of Discipline Hall. Jordan is surprised by how large the room is with just a few pieces of furniture in it. It has a couple of stools at various heights, another padded table, and another bent over bench. These pieces are placed in various areas which gives the room plenty of floor space and makes it very open.

"These are the stools I use for over the knee spankings. I also use them for kneeling spankings.

That padded table I use to lay students flat on their tummy with their fanny up. I may also have them lay on their back as I lift their legs up and spank them." Kate explains effortlessly in a very professional and matter of fact kind of way.

Jordan feels a little jittery inside, maybe a slight bit of fear or maybe the feeling is that he's getting really turned on. The most notable difference in this room are the large mirrors on every wall. This makes the walls look like a dance studio or exercise room. Jordan looks and turns in all directions as he sees both of their reflections from every angle.

"Yep, I added the mirrors." Principal Kate proudly claims.

"I feel it's important for someone to see themselves when they are getting spanked. They can see everything from every angle. The look on their faces right down to the redness of their cheeks."

Kate further explains and goes into her research and fact mode.

"Being embarrassed and vulnerable is a big part of correcting bad behavior. Trust me it works."

Jordan is now all out fully and intensely, turned on. His erection is very close to making his dick come thru the top of his jeans.

"I re-configured these rooms to have plenty of space, especially this main room. There have been times that multiple offenders and/or multiple teachers need to be in here."

She also tells him that this is her favorite room to discipline naughty students. Aside from the mirrors she loves having enough room to move freely. She continues by saying that once she gets a student in this room it doesn't matter if they try to move around or get away from her.

"When that happens I can still pursue them and put them back in position without bumping into everything. It's kind of like being in a ring and pursuing your opponent." She says as her eyes quickly wander to the view in the mirror scoping out his beautiful ass once again.

Principal Kate doesn't know why she's talking so freely and in more detail regarding spankings with Jordan. She never talked so openly or so effortlessly like that with any student in her 4 years as principal.

A good number of attending students have no experience with corporal punishment especially bare bottom spankings. Usually a quick mention and tour of Discipline Hall is enough for her to sense some fear in their eyes and a tremble in their voice. Many students won't even see the inside of Discipline Hall throughout their four years here at The Academy.

However, with Jordan it's definitely different. He's more mature, more calm and collected. She doesn't get a sense that he is afraid or shocked. He seems to be un-phased and just taking it all in. Of course she doesn't know that he is insanely turned on and that her tour just continues to drive him nuts. She points to some of the grips that could extend down from the ceiling. She mentions this is where she may instruct a student to hold.

By now Jordan's dick is hard beyond belief and actually uncomfortable. She continues, making mention of the student handbook and confirms that he has read and understands the guidelines pertaining to spanking and corporal punishment used at the school. She specifically makes sure that he fully comprehends the section explaining the different levels of spankings from a level 5 preventative maintenance spanking, up to a level 10 with the reform school strap and/or wooden paddle. Jordan fully understands and shakes his head yes.

She then walks over to the closet by the wall and opens it. Inside there is a vast display of implements from leather straps to wooden paddles in various sizes. She pulls out the reform school strap and proceeds to tell Jordan that this is her favorite to use when dealing with misbehavior. She starts to walk around the room tapping the large strap in her hand. She is now making it very obvious that she's staring him down and trying to get a response from him. Jordan never looks away as he maintains eye contact with her the whole time. She notices that he doesn't gasp or seem embarrassed or give any of the usual reactions that students usually do. He doesn't seem shocked by any of the furniture or implements. He seems like he is familiar with all of this. Actually, he seems like he has experience.

She then tries a little different approach and gives him a taste of her stern tone, "Let me assure you darling that I won't hesitate to yank your pants down and apply this strap to your bare bottom if you misbehave. Is that understood?"

Jordan now crazy fucking turned on manages a response with no waiver or tremble in his voice at all. "Yes, I absolutely understand Principal Kate." While on the inside he's trying to do all he can to take his mind off of his huge hard on.

Principal Kate realizes she might of gotten carried away and may have come across a bit too stern. She then composes herself and continues to clarify the school policy and that a student can always opt out of the consent form they signed regarding corporal punishment. She explains this only happened once or twice since the schools inception, however, if that is the case, then the student will be not be spanked and will be immediately suspended from school. Choosing this option, they would have 2 days to reconsider, if not they are expelled plain and simple. They would then have to pack their belongings and leave the campus. Kate then returns the strap back into the closet and walks with Jordan back to her office.

CHAPTER SEVEN

◆ ◆ ◆

They settle back in her office and Jordan is still pretty turned on, although the walk back helped his hard on subside a little. He is still dying to know more about her and isn't ready for his orientation with her to end yet.

Specifically, he wants to know more about her spanking experience. He knows it's more than just a job for her. He can absolutely sense it. She's way too passionate about it. It's a lifestyle for her and it's a part of her sexy and kinky nature.

He's witnessed it before and he's very in touch with his own sexuality. People that are into it and "non-vanilla" can just feed off each other. It's kind of a sixth sense you get when you find someone that equally loves and understands the kink, the control, the mind/body connection, and the power exchange dynamic. So whether she knows it or not, Principal Kate has already shown him a side of her that goes way beyond a principal correcting behavior… She uncovered a bit of her soul and he plans on unwrapping all of it. He begins to ponder how to find out more without being so obvious or so perverted. He quickly asks her about where she attended college and what her major was. Hopefully this will lead her to uncover more.

"I majored in psychology with a minor in sports medicine at a private college similar to this." she replies. Jordan is still trying to coax and find out more from her. He asks her if she worked at the school or maintained a part-time job elsewhere while attending. This approach works perfectly and he gets exactly what he's looking for.

She proceeds to tell Jordan the story of her college years in Texas as a live-in nanny to two unruly teenagers. She gives him all of the details he needed to hear. How she spanked them and how they quickly changed their behavior. She also tells him how they would monitor themselves and actually ask her for a preventative maintenance spanking if they felt they were getting off track. Once again, she makes it clear that she added these type of PM spankings to this school. She reiterates that any member of the staff can give this type of spanking to the student. All they have to do is ask.

He's now rock hard again but manages to respond in agreement, "Yeah, I totally get that. It's an effective way to increase focus and even relieve stress. It's also a way to be held accountable. It actually shows self respect to realize that you are getting off track and you want to correct it before it gets worse."

Jordan was spot on and he knew how fellow kinksters feed off each other. His intelligent response back makes her sport a twinkle in her eyes, "You are way beyond your 18 years Jordan." She says.

"I'm actually 19 on Monday, the first day of school ma' am." Jordan replied.

"Still, remember what I said. You have intelligence and street smarts." She replies and then flirts with her eyes in a quick up and down motion. She then turns on a cute smirk and says, "So if you ever need a spanking just come to me and ask. I'll be more than happy to properly introduce my hand to your cheeks."

Principal Kate was now actually flirting with him. She knew it wholeheartedly. Never, ever in her years as Principal did she talk like this with a student. She hadn't even talked with this type of sexual energy with anyone else in years. For some reason Jordan brought this side of her out with even more intensity. An intensity that she knew was going down a dangerous yet intoxi-cating path. A sexual tension so thick it caused her to say to herself... Kensington, snap the fuck out of this!

The orientation with Principal Kate Ken-sington came to an end and Jordan's head, as well as, his dick were swelled and reeling with emo-tions. He immediately went back to his dorm room still so turned on by Principal Kate and everything about her. Her looks, her confidence, her nurturing then stern but sexy side. Basically all she encompassed.

Without waiting a minute longer he strips down and gets into a steamy hot shower. He starts stroking himself as he lathers soap all over his dick. It feels beyond amazing to him as he closes his eyes and pictures Kate doing everything under the sun to him. Then he pictures himself turning the tables on her. He can hear her moans echoing thru his ears as he totally dominates her. With those thoughts in mind he strokes himself harder into elation. He totally climaxes and finally re-lieves himself of the hard on that had been en-gulfing his every thought.

Jordan Thompson harboring a few secrets of his own, manages to keep a calm and collected exterior yet inside he has an extremely creative, dominant, and erotic wild side. It's far from van-illa and it's just a matter of time before it truly emerges. He now retreats to his bed feeling completely spent. He starts reflecting on his full week of orientation and the annual student kick- off dance party tomorrow night. He thinks about the female staff that are all very attractive, as well as, some of the incredibly hot girls he has seen walking around campus. Most of all he thinks about Principal Kate and how he would love to get her alone and give her a taste of his world and all he knows and loves. He gets a comforting feeling that maybe she might just be the one to fully understand his hidden kinks and secrets.

Jordan ponders all of this as his mind finally starts to quiet. Then he slowly closes his eyes and drifts off to sleep.

The Academy series continues with book 2 of the story as everyone is excited about attending the popular meet and greet, annual kick-off dance party. An event some students wish they had not attended!

The Academy
Kick-Off Dance
Book 2

CHAPTER ONE

◆ ◆ ◆

It's Friday morning and Jordan is slowly waking up and opening his eyes. He reaches down and starts to touch his already stiff cock. It's the same thing he does just about every morning, however, today it's even more intense. Today, his dick is as big as a Louisville Slugger baseball bat. Still fresh on his mind are thoughts of Principal Kate and the things they discussed yesterday during his orientation and tour of The Academy. So far, he loves everything about the unique, top rated private boarding college. His private condo style dorm is beautiful, the recreation and fitness center is state of the art, and the all female faculty are incredibly attractive. He is really looking forward to the start of the semester on Monday and The Annual Student Kick-Off Dance tonight but right now every inch of the morning wood he's feeling is dedicated to Principal Kate.

It was quite a conversation during his 2 plus hour discussion and orientation with her to say the least. There was just something about her that drove him nuts. Actually, it was everything about her. First off, the way she looked and rocked that tight business skirt and blouse she was wearing. The way her hips were so curvy and flowed up to her thin waist. Those big green eyes that are just about the same color and size of his. And damn that ass!

He also loved the way she carried herself. She had a great vibe of being warm, nurturing, cool, and confident. Then he was absolutely amazed at how quick her tone changed and became more serious as she went over the student handbook, school rules, and consequences for misbehavior. The moment she talked in detail about bare bottom spankings is when he got turned on beyond belief. His dick was rock hard sitting there listening to her explain how she was spanked bare bottom a lot as a teenager. She even elaborated and told him how she worked as a live-in nanny for 2 unruly teens and how she had no hesitation in giving them bare bottom spankings when they misbehaved. Right then and there he just about blew a gasket. However, the kicker yesterday was when she told him that she still gives bare bottom spankings frequently here at the school and capped it off by giving him the campus tour which included Discipline Hall. Yep, that's when his mind was officially fully blown!

It's no wonder that he's waking up with his dick extra hard. He now starts to get that tingle in his body as his mind connects with images of Principal Kate doing everything imaginable to him. Without hardly stroking himself, he's unable to hold it in any longer and he climaxes as sperm shoots up onto his abs. He feels totally relieved with a new sense of calmness. He gets out of bed, cleans himself up, and then comes right back and lays down again. The orgasm absolutely took the edge off and now he starts to fully take in the beauty of his bedroom. The school decorated these dorm rooms beautifully, and he further embellished it by bringing some of his own items like his special sheets, cool pillows, a stereo, and some nice lamps. He is really excited for the new energy and size of this beautiful bedroom, as well as, for the amazing condo style dorm.

The kitchen was the smallest room but it was nice and fully equipped. The living room was large and open with a beautiful leather sectional and 50 inch flat screen TV. He was already conjuring up kinky thoughts of the action this new place would see. He felt really happy and welcomed here at the small private college and classes didn't even start yet.

He started reflecting on all the orientation

meetings and the interesting conversations he had this week with the women faculty. They all seemed to have a certain warmth about them that he really loved. It's kind of a caring, family type of vibe here at this school, at least so far that's the vibe he gets.

The thoughts of orientation week are now re-playing in his mind. It was sure an interesting and eventful 3 days. As he lays in bed, he begins to reflect on all of them. He starts with his first orientation meeting with the founders Ms. Marilyn and Ms. Marj on Tuesday. He visited Ms. Marj in the morning and then Ms. Marilyn in the afternoon. He thinks about their farms and the farmhouses they reside in and how he met some of the students that are interning and residing there. He remembers thinking both sisters seem kind of cool in their own way. He connected a bit more with Ms. Marilyn because she reminded him of one of his older Aunts. Of course to an 18 year old anyone in the vicinity of age 50 is old and anyone beyond age 60 is ancient. So to Jordan, Ms. Marilyn was actually old, but she did have some vibrancy in her. She was definitely a hard worker, probably rigid and stuck in her ways, but yet very warm, old fashioned, and traditional. He summed her up as the kind of woman that would bake you an apple pie or some oatmeal raisin cookies for no reason. He also fell in love with the 2 dogs they both owned, and he promised to visit them frequently to walk and play with them.

Laying there, he now thinks about his Wednesday morning orientation meeting with Ms. Carrie Ann. The thing he remembers most about her is her tits. He replays walking into her office and the moment she stood up from behind her desk. He remembers thinking to himself, holy shit Jessica Rabbit with brown hair! He tried not to look at her cleavage and did everything he could to maintain eye contact when they were talking. She is one beautiful and voluptuous teacher as her tits now occupy his mind. He guesses that she's probably late 40's or early 50's. He recalls their conversation about nutrition and sharing fitness routines. Jordan mentioned how he loves to jump rope in between sets of weightlifting, and she shared her love for spinning classes and cross-fit. She has dark olive skin that made him wonder if she's from Columbia, Brazil, or Spain. All that was cool, however, what he remembers most about her are her big beautiful tits.

His Wednesday afternoon was hectic and booked solid but he is still able to recall it in detail. First off, his early afternoon orientation was with Ms. Brooke and then late afternoon he met with Ms. Paige. He reflects on how they both were pretty chill ladies. He guessed they were mid 40's but both looked active and in good shape.

They must do Pilates classes or yoga all the

time he thought. They have that Zen type of vibe going on. They also remind him of his favorite news casters on TV and some popular talk show hosts. He specifically remembers how they were very organized and kind of scripted, but yet they were still really warm and left him feeling wel-comed.

His thoughts then shifted to the meetings he had yesterday with Ms. Jenn and of course Principal Kate. It is one Thursday he will always remember. He thinks about the morning orienta-tion with Ms. Jenn. He has the same thought right now as he did yesterday. Holy Fuck, Ms. Jenn is smoking hot! She reminded him of the other hot women named Jennifer that he's fantasized about. Jennifer Love Hewitt, Jennifer Garner, Jennifer Lopez, Jennifer Aniston, all came to his mind yes-terday. For some reason she even reminded him of Jennifer Brooks, who isn't as widely known as the other Jennifer's.

Only the true spank-a-holics would know that Jennifer Brooks was a very popular spank-ing model and actress. Anyway, maybe it was just the name Jennifer that set him off. Regardless, his mind was like a runaway "kink" train. Aside from being incredibly attractive, the best thing about Ms. Jenn is that she loves football. What a woman! She talked football with him for at least an hour. They talked about their favorite NFL teams and players. Her team of course is the New England

Patriots and it was obvious she wanted to have her next kid with Tom Brady. She knew way too many facts about him especially his diet. He remembers her listing all the foods Tom terrific eats and avoids.

Ms. Jenn also talked proudly about her kids. She mentioned her son that is in 8th grade and is on the middle school football team. He plays quarterback of course. Her daughter is her oldest child, starting her first year of high school. She is a cheerleader and also plays piano. She ended the football talk by sharing that her youngest son plays peewee football in a league every Saturday. They also talked about how she loves weight training and eating sushi. She gave him the impression that she must be a really cool mom that's strict and formal when she has to be, but mostly caring and very understanding. That's the vibe he got from her. The totally hot, caring, football mom.

On Thursday he also met Nurse Madison but only briefly since she was swamped with paperwork. His mind starts to recap how crazy, busy she was in getting ready for the first day on Monday. He remembers how she apologized a few times for being so busy but yet she still managed to give him a few minutes of her time. This time of year right before the new semester starts, is always her busiest time she told him. That was obvious as she was drowning in folders and piles of papers stacked on her desk.

Nurse Madison is another very attractive, slightly older woman maybe around late 40's he guessed. Regardless, she is beautiful and he remembers how toned her arms are. It's obvious that staying physically fit and in-shape is a huge priority here at The Academy. This must be a requirement for the faculty he thought. They must live by the old fashion saying "lead by example". Needless to say, Jordan thought he'd died and gone to heaven with so many attractive and personable teachers.

However, he was very much alive as his dick can attest to. They made small talk for a few minutes and she smiled and said thank you when Jordan complimented her on her toned arms. He also mentioned how every staff member he met is in great physical shape. The pretty nurse responded by telling him that it's a requirement and part of the job. She also admitted to him that all of the faculty are committed fitness buffs.

"All of us make exercise and proper nutrition part of our lifestyle here and at home with our families." She added. He reflected on her apologizing again for being so busy but reassured him that they will have plenty of time to talk during his school physical. Her exact words now echoed in his mind as he was laying in bed.

"Don't worry honey, I should be contacting

you in the next month or so once I get caught up with this paperwork." He specifically remembers how warm her voice was.

The image of her standing up and extending her hand to say a formal goodbye yesterday now comes into his head. He remembers taking notice of her thin, long, pretty fingers, specifically the index finger on her right hand. He couldn't help that his eyes held a slightly longer than usual stare at her fingers as his kinky mind went into over-drive. He remembers his exact thought yesterday was… I can't wait to feel that finger in my ass!

Jordan wasn't the only one staring as he re-calls some of the looks Nurse Madison gave back to him as well. She also held a slightly longer than normal stare at him when she stood up and faced him. This was clear when she give him a quick look up and down then commented to him that he has a beautiful physique. He thought… hmmm, that little twinkle in her eye could be her thinking about examining me. He vividly recalls the cute little smirk on her face as she said, "I promise you sweetie, we will have plenty of time to talk. Your orientation with me will be just as thorough as your school physical."

There is no freaking way he could ever for-get those words. His disk just wont let him. Yester-day, Jordan's mind was already a step ahead of hers as he thought to himself.…

FUCK, hurry up and schedule my physical!

He's now laughing to himself as he remembers walking with a hard on to his very last orientation with Principal Kate.

CHAPTER TWO

❖ ❖ ❖

S o here he is, fully awake but still laying in bed with his mind reflecting back on all the orientation meetings from Tuesday, Wednesday, and Thursday. He is totally taken back and reminiscing about just how attractive and warm the entire female faculty is.

These thoughts make his cock rise again to another epic erection. He reaches down and this time immediately starts stroking himself as he becomes even more turned on mentally and physically. Numerous kinky thoughts are playing over and over in his mind and they're creating one steamy, sexy movie. He thinks about Nurse Madison's long, pretty, fingers, Ms. Carrie Ann's tits, and Ms. Jenn's overall hot mom vibe. Then of course the thoughts of Principal Kate come thru loud and clear. Her voice begins to resonate within him again. Her big green eyes looking him over and actually looking right thru him. This time his mind creates an intense movie with vivid images of all the things he wants to do to her.

He's now hearing the sexy moans of her voice clearly in his ears. This was all it took and he totally loses it. Laying right there in bed within all of 2 minutes after stroking himself, he totally climaxes as sperm once again shoots up onto his killer abs.

Needless to say, Friday morning is off to a great start. Fresh from just pleasuring himself thinking about every kinky scenario under the sun, Jordan now gets moving with a spring in his step. He puts in a killer workout and comes back to his dorm for shower number 2.

Outside it's a beautiful 80 degree sun filled September day as summer is still in full force. Inspired by the weather, he puts on his swim shorts, tank-top, and heads to Kentville Falls state park. This is one beautiful state park with wild flowers, picnic tables, hiking trails, and a natural waterfall that gathers below into several rock pools.

It's an extremely popular place in this area of the state and people love spending the day swimming and just hanging out in the water. He arrives and immediately sets out a towel and takes in some sun. Feeling totally relaxed, he gets in a short nap and then wakes up thinking about the kick-off dance tonight. He's looking forward to making new friends and meeting other students attending the school this year. He is also looking forward to seeing some of his attractive teachers again, especially Principal Kate. As he feels the warmth of the sun, his mind is on-track to create another uncomfortable hard on for him. He quickly tries to prevent it and decides to head to the falls and cool off.

The water is cold but absolutely refreshing, as he plunges right in. It's a great hangout and in the short time he's standing in the waist deep water he manages to have several interesting conversations with some locals and some weekend visitors. Needless to say, Jordan's physique also manages to draw attention from onlookers.

Ms. Jenn and Principal Kate just finished their noon workout and are enjoying their day off before having to attend the kick-off dance tonight. They decide to grab some lunch, take it to the falls, and enjoy this spectacular September day. Aside from being peers, they've become very close friends over a short time. Kate constantly tells Jenn that she loves spending time with her and her sense of humor is intoxicating. She has a way of making her laugh so hard that sometimes she can't even catch her breath. The two of them have their lunch in hand, enter the scenic park, and start walking toward an open picnic table.

Kate asks, "How's that one over there? It has some shade and some sun."

Perfect!" Jenn replies, "We'll have a chance to catch up. It feels good not to be on Mom duty. Who's watching Josh today, your mom?"

"Yeah, they might come by for a swim. She was taking him for a haircut first. She is such a big help."

"That kid of yours is the cutest thing I've ever seen, Kate. I adore him."

"Well, he sure loves you too Aunty Jenn. He loves going over to your house and playing with your kids also."

"He makes me just melt, especially when he calls me Aunty Jenn. So are you ready for the kick-off dance tonight?" Jenn asks.

Kate responds, "Yep, it's always a great event. Let's just keep our eyes open for underage drinking and pot smoking. Those are the 2 big things that happen at this dance. So, by the way, where is Steven and the kids?"

"He took them up to Vermont to spend

time with their grandparents. I'm kid-less and hubby-less the entire weekend. Woooo Hoooo." Jenn cheers.

"Let's catch up... How are things with you guys? Should I even ask…. Are they any better?" Kate hesitantly asks.

Jenn takes a deep breath and let's it all come out, "Honestly Kate, nothing's changed. I tell you everything so you already know all I'm going thru. In fact, you are the only one that knows and can even relate to it. I have zero secrets with you and I love being able to confide in you. You're a true friend."

"I feel the same about you, Jenn. I tell you everything and you are such an amazing friend. I've been there and I went thru everything you are feeling until I finally had to make a move."

"I could never make a move right now. The kids would freak and they would hate me. Plus, I'm not sure that would be the right move." Jenn replies.

"I totally get it. You have 3 kids to consider and I only had Joshua. Plus, he was just a toddler, so it was easier for me to move on and let my marriage go." Kate responds and gives her a hug.

"I've just got to have my physical needs met.
Steven and I are so different in that depart-

ment. I mean, he never was kinky so I guess I just put that part of me aside all these years. Now it's come to the surface and it's consuming me. Regardless, he just doesn't have it in him to go there and be that way." Jenn replies in frustration.

"I know you've been trying to see if he can get into it. How about my last suggestions? Did you try to get him to go there mentally first? Ya' know, tease him, role play and see if he catches on." Kate asks.

"Totally, I tried everything, Kate. I even put on the policewoman uniform and thought maybe he wants me to take control, dominate him, and lead the way. Nope, didn't work.... he freaked when I put on the latex gloves and told him I was going to cuff him and strip search him. So that was a complete bust… no pun intended." Jenn gives a disappointed chuckle.

"Whew Jenn, I remember how you look in that uniform. That's the one we bought at the flea market right? The authentic one with the real patches sewn in it?"

"Yeppers…. that's the one, the real deal. You even helped me pick out more accessories that day, the cuffs, the old walkie-talkie. Remember, we even went to CVS for the gloves and Vaseline?"

"Sure do, I totally remember and I know that uniform won't go to waste. I can relate so much to the disappointment that you're feeling. I have many outfits in my closet that haven't seen the light of day yet. All I know is, Officer Jenn will make one hot policewoman and it's sure to be an amazing role play scenario. Hell, when do you want to arrest me?" Kate laughs with a nervous energy and continues to edge her on.

"Damn, thinking of you in that uniform and taking on that role suddenly got me all tingly Jenn."

Jenn laughing a little and giving it right back, "Only if you promise that we can play that scenario in your exercise room. I love those big mirrors on your walls. We'll get to see every angle and take it all in. Actually, you kind of made that room look like Discipline Hall."

Kate laughs with her, "Yeah, that was the idea. Make a kink room in my home that's disguised to look like an exercise room. The only exercise it sees is kink."

Jenn laughs, "I think it's brilliant, Kate. You have this large room with some mats, different benches, the massage table, those TRX hanging things, and those mirrors. No one would ever suspect what you really use it for. I mean look at you.... They just think, God she must exercise 10 hours a day with a body like that."

"Awe, what a nice compliment." Kate replies and hugs her.

"That room continues to work as long as I keep my props locked away in that storage trunk in the closet. Plus, I keep that room locked all the time and Josh knows he isn't allowed to play in it. That's why he has his own play room upstairs with all his toys." Kate laughs and flashes her a cute smirk.

"Well, your an amazing mom and it shows. So you have a kinky side... big deal.... Your not married and nothing is stopping you from enjoying that side as much as you want. I wish I had the total freedom to explore more of that side and dive into all my fantasies. It would just feel so free." Jenn continues to vent.

"Honestly Kate, if it wasn't for you I would be even more of a hot mess. There's no doubt I would be full on cheating and still having an affair. It would just be a matter of time before I got caught and everything would fall apart. Steven, the kids, our home, it would all crash and burn. You satisfy that need and you've helped me more than you'll ever know. Plus, I love experiencing this kinky stuff with you. I've never been so open with anyone in all my life and you totally understand the kink inside of me. You help me bring it to life."

Kate just listens as Jenn goes on.

"It's so nice to know that I can tell you anything and we can talk about these things. I'm so much more in tune with myself as a whole. My mind, my body, my fantasies, and my needs. Finally, I totally understand it all. My sexuality has really come alive over this last year or so and it's all thanks to you. I give you all the credit." Jenn admits.

"Thanks babe, but I can't take all the credit. You probably always had this creative mindset and all this kinkiness is naturally within you. I guess it just came to the surface and really woke up. Anyway, you know I love our friendship, it's truly special and it's one that I treasure." Kate replies and continues.

"Who cares if we help fulfill some of each others fantasies with a little kink now and then?" Kate laughs and squints her eyes, shooting her a sexy look.

"And, we can always adjust it or stop it entirely. I never want it to get in the way of anything or get too complicated." Kate assures her.

Jenn responds quickly with a little panic, "It won't get in the way at all. I need it, Kate... I mean, it's an escape that I really love and I feel I need it to keep me sane. Besides, why would it get in the way? It's not like we're a lesbian couple wanting to get married to each other. We both love cock way too much for that!"

Kate laughs and spits out her ice tea in mid sip. "Ow that hurt…. that went right up my nose, Jenn." She continues laughing as she wipes her face with a napkin.

"We play such an important part in each others lives. We're the best of friends that enjoy each others company and we share the same kinky pleasures. Plus, we both hold each other account-able and that's a perfect balance. It can't get any better than this, unless we add a couple more cocks, some big biceps, and a few more lips to the mix once in a while." Jenn explains in her warped way.

Kate now laughing uncontrollably, "Jenn STOP! You're killing me. I can't catch my breath."

"I didn't mean it to be funny. I really meant it." Jenn giggles and then asks.

"Hey, when is the next impact or rope event in the city? We need to go."

Kate replies, "I haven't been on the website in a while but I'll check and we'll definitely go. I think there is a weekend spanking event in New Jersey sometime in late fall. They rent a hotel and set up the rooms with various themes. They do a lot of role playing and encourage everyone to bring various outfits. That could be a blast, so I'll double check on that as well."

Jenn replies with excitement, "I'm all in! I haven't been on the website or updated my profile either. I'll make it a point to check the information too."

"Jenn, are you sure Steven wouldn't attend any of these type of events? I mean maybe he would find it arousing to go and just watch." Kate asks.

"I highly doubt it, he's just so vanilla and has zero creativity. He would totally judge me and think it's stupid or taboo. He doesn't understand that I need to satisfy these desires in me and play out some of these fantasies. He'll think it's just about sex and we know it's not about that at all. It's about the mind/body connection, subspace, the power exchange and so much more. Someone that isn't open will never understand it." She goes on and continues to vent.

"I want to embrace the creativity and feel uninhibited. I don't want to look back on my life and have regrets. Let's face it Kate, we're both vibrant, attractive, and in great health so now is the time. I have to concentrate on myself and experiencing all these things. There is so much I want to do and so much I love to do, it's just not with him." Jenn shares again with frustration.

"Jenn, have you thought about asking him for an open relationship or at least some form of it? Kate asks and then further explains when Jenn raises her eyebrow in disbelief.

"I know it's not for everyone and it's not all about sex. You can even have some limits like no full on sex with anyone else. It may work Jenn, since you already have a great foundation and all you're looking for is more physical excitement.... More freedom, more creativity... right?" Kate reiterates.

Jenn responds with a sarcastic giggle, "Oh hell no! Steven? My vanilla Steven? In an open relationship? There's not a chance in hell he would go for that." Jenn goes on.

"That's why I cheated. It wasn't about sex, I just needed to feel that desire and creative energy. I needed to feel something emotionally, as well as, physically that he doesn't give me. Kate, sometimes I want to be dominated and sometimes I want to dominate. I have multiple sides of me just like you. Sometimes I want to top... sometimes I want to bottom... I want to use toys, handcuffs, rope, blindfolds, and have them be used on me."

Kate nods her head in agreement, "Yep, you got it bad... It's the curse... The kink curse just like me."

Jenn laughs and continues to spill her soul, "OMG, the kink curse. That's priceless Kate Kensington... haha. Seriously, I just love to feel that total mind/body connection. I love to role play, I love toys, and of course I want to spank and get spanked. It's a huge part of me. I love it, need it, and I don't want to hide it anymore. I can't hide it anymore."

Kate replies in agreement, "It's a huge part of me also, Jenn. I understand this more than you know. That's what ended my marriage. I did actually come out and ask for an open relationship. I was completely honest... I showed him my profiles on the kink sites and I even took him to some events. He tried at first to understand it, but it was short lived. Within two months he couldn't deal with it. So that was the catalyst for us to go our separate ways."

"Kate, are we weird? I mean we both love all this kinky shit and we don't feel right unless we get it. We're both loving moms, we have great families, and we're dedicated business professionals, so isn't that enough? Why do we desire it so much? Is there something wrong with us?" Jenn questions.

Kate takes Jenn's hand, "No babe, you're not weird and I'm not weird.... Well OK, let's just say you're not weird." Jenn laughs and listens to her friend go on.

"Jenn, just think about it for a moment. We are both in total control 99 percent of the time in our everyday lives. The demands on us from our kids, to run our houses, to maintain our jobs, do all the errands, grocery shopping, laundry, it's fucking crazy."

"This stress and these demands continue to build and build with more being piled on our plates." Kate goes on.

"So it makes perfect sense that once in a while we need a release, an escape. Some people turn to drugs or alcohol, which ends up hurting themselves and their loved ones. This is something we do openly, and it's consensual. Maybe we want someone else to take control, or we want to experience a different dynamic to get that release. The only way I can further explain it, is that we are both just really in touch with our sexuality. We actually know what we need to be happy."

Jenn just listens as Kate further explains, "We totally crave the intensity and the rush from having a kinky, fetish, lifestyle. It gives us this release emotionally and physically. Plus, now that we've experienced it, we refuse to settle for vanilla or anything that's boring and routine." Kate replies.

Jenn feeling so relieved lets it all out, "Steven, won't do any of this kinky shit. He rarely goes down on me. He just goes straight into fuck mode. Forget about asking him to tie me, use toys on me, finger my ass, or get rough. Plus, he won't spank me and sometimes I just want to get spanked…

hard…. I mean, really spanked like the way you do it Kate." She says with a slight smile and continues talking.

"I mean let's face it, we give enough spankings so we know about having that power and authority, but I think it's a huge turn on to be held accountable and to get your ass tanned once in while. Am I right?"

Kate responds, "Works for me". They both laugh and Kate responds.

"Actually, you are spot on, Jenn. I love to get it just as much as I love to give it. You already know that it's so much more than just physical. It takes that special mindset and dynamic for someone to take that control away from you and make you feel vulnerable. That's why when you find that perfect someone that shares the same kinks, it creates a very special and unique bond."

"I love having that bond with you Kate. You get me and I get you. Plus, it's kind of easy for us to keep it low key. I love that I can just ask you for a play date."

Kate bursts out laughing again, "OMG a play date… that's classic, Jenn. Two mom's having a play date… haha."

Jenn laughs along and admits, "That was kinda funny but I love the way you spank me and will hold me accountable if I ask. Not to mention, I love switching with you and reddening that beautiful ass of yours too."

Kate confirms, "It's a huge turn-on knowing I have a true friend that I can turn to that would do this stuff to me and with me. Not to mention, she's quite beautiful, you would really like her." Kate's joke catches Jenn off guard and keeps her smiling.

"Jenn, I know I was hesitant and worried in the beginning. I remember telling you how I was afraid about having this type of kink relationship with you. I mean, I wanted it so badly but I didn't want to risk our amazing friendship... and we work together. Then I took a breath and realized that it was all in my head and I was making it out to be more than it is. It's just two grown women who are good friends, that enjoy exploring each others mind and body. The fact is, we both handle it really well and it doesn't get in the way at all. We're both committed moms and we always put our families first. I guess it's just nice to know that we can get some of our needs and fantasies met with each other."

Jenn agrees, "Kate, I think everyone at work must also have a kinky side. We would never work at The Academy if it wasn't a part of us and it didn't come naturally. However, I'm proud of the fact that none of us cross the line and we never let it interfere with our professional duties. We know the difference and our no nonsense policy is a major reason this school has such a prestigious reputation. Still, all of this stuff is a huge part of us and our sexuality. That adrenaline rush you get when you have to administer discipline for misbehavior... We know it's natural, but we also embrace and enjoy having that power and authority. Plus, let's face it, we're good at correcting bad behavior. I know that everyone here from Marj, Marilyn, Brooke all enjoy having this authority as well. You can just see it... it's a part of them too and I'm sure they have some kinkiness inside of them."

Kate shakes her head in agreement, "Of course they do, at least in some way".

"And Maddy, for sure is a kinky fucking freak!" Jenn makes Kate laugh again and continues.

"Check this out Kate.... Remember last year when I felt a cold coming on and thought it could develop into the flu? Well, Maddy came over and made a house call. She gave me a full examination and I mean a FULL examination. She took her time, didn't rush one minute, and had me naked the entire time. I got a sense that she really enjoyed looking at my body and having that power dynamic to freely examine me..."

Kate suddenly interjects, "Ummm... duh... Jenn? Newsflash..Who wouldn't enjoy examining you?

"Seriously Kate, in that moment I felt it

and I knew Maddy had a kinky side. I just got a vibe, a sense that she loved having that authority and dynamic, at least with me she did. So, like I was saying before I was rudely interrupted..." Jenn flashes Kate a stern but comical look and continues.

"Maddy really took her time as her fingers probed every part of my body inside and out. Kate, WTF? All this for a cold or flu?" Her and Kate both laugh together.

"C'mon, in my entire life there has never been a doctor or nurse that took that long to examine me. Plus, it was the way she looked at me, positioned me, and fingered me. She just knew it was going to feel good. She turned me over and fingered the fuck out of my ass and it was such a turn on. I mean, I can't say it helped my coughing or sore throat, but hey, I like a little ass action... So, there was no way I was going to stop her!"

Again Kate can't help but burst out in laughter as Jenn continues to further explain.

"When she took that glove off and told me to turn over on my back so she can examine my vagina. I was total putty in her hands. She actually reached for another glove and went thru the motions, but I'm willing to bet that she didn't even put it on. I actually felt every bit of her fingers and once they plunged deep into my pussy I couldn't help it, and I had an orgasm. She just smiled and said, "It's OK Jenn, that's natural. It shows you're a perfectly healthy woman aside from fighting off this cold."

"Holy Fuck, Jenn! I've never experienced that from any nurse or doctor." Kate replies.

"Well I did, and then she gave me a shot... stuck that needle in my ass!"

"I would of enjoyed it much more if she gave me the injection before I came." Jenn adds.

Kate goes into a crazy laugh and once again snorts her ice tea in mid sip, "Shit Jenn, you have to warn me before I take a sip."

Jenn now looking around the park comments, "Damn Kate, is it me or are there just a whole bunch of snacks here today?"

"Snacks?... Haha, OMG you're killing me, Jenn."

"I mean, look at that guy over there with his little girl. That's not a dad body!"

"And that guy in the jeans with the blue shirt... Nah, scratch that... I think he's eyeing that dad guy I just mentioned. I don't think he's into women at all."

"Jenn! You can't just judge people." Kate still laughing.

Jenn gasps, "Holy Fuck, Captain America!"

"Who?" Kate looks around.

"That guy in the water with the baseball cap turned backwards, and the orange swim shorts."

"I still don't see Captain America." Kate adds.

"Kate.. him over there! We have to see if his face looks as amazing as his back and shoulders. Let's go to that other picnic table that's closer and in the shade. I'll make some hand gestures like the sun is too strong and it's in our eyes. This way it wont look so obvious, even though I'm a complete perv and my hormones are freaking out right now."

"You're in rare form today." Kate says with a smirk.

Jenn continues, "That's it, move out of the water Captain. Let me see that ass of yours!"

Kate laughing again, "Jenn! What's gotten into you?"

"Ha, sorry Kate, but he looks like a guy that can put me in my place. C'mon don't you think he's hot?"

Kate reasons, "Well, I'm an ass girl as you know, so I'm waiting to see him come further out of the water. Then I'll give you my verdict."

Jenn adds more of her humor, "Yeah, watch him have a totally flat ass! He's probably a preppy, arrogant, Wall street executive that walks like he's constipated."

Kate responds, "Jenn!"

Jenn continues her rant, "C'mon big boy.. back it up, back it up, lemme see that ass..." A minute or so later the hot guy takes a few steps backward into knee deep water.

Jenn freaks, "OK Houston, we have the moon in sight!

There Kate, that's an ass for you... I told you he would have a great ass... Happy now?"

Kate still laughing manages to get serious and focus, "Yep, my verdict is in... Captain America and whoever else you think he looks like, it doesn't matter. All I know is that is a fucking snack and I would devour that!"

Jenn approves, "Now that's the Kate Kensington I know. Just be a good friend and let me devour it with you.... OK, OK, or at least let me watch?"

Kate kneels over with laughter, "Jenn! I can't even... I have no words..."

"I want to see what his face looks like. I can't tell from here. C'mon Kate, let's go feel the

Robin Fairchild

water."

CHAPTER THREE

◆ ◆ ◆

As good as that idea sounded the two of them remain at their picnic table. They carry on for another 10 minutes discussing Mr. Hotness standing in the knee deep water with his ass to them, looking like some kind of "snack".

Feeling anxious Jenn suggests once again, "Kate C'mon, come with me to the water."

"Sorry Jenn, I'm frozen in thought right now. His ass has all my attention." Kate adds.

He then turns and looks around the park giving them a slight view of his face although his sunglasses cover most of it.

"Kate, from what I can see he's really cute. I'm digging the bad boy kind of look with the backwards baseball cap, the shades, and that five o'clock shadow thingy. He's rocking it!" Jenn replies.

Just then the good looking stranger walks out of the water in the direction of his towel on the grass. He notices the two pretty women and flashes them a smile as he waves. Then he starts to walk over to their picnic table. Suddenly, the two of them look at each other and think WTF?

"Hey Miss Jenn, Hey Principal Kate, nice seeing you both. How are you?"

"Jordan, ummm... Hi... sorry, I didn't recognize you with the cap and shades on." Kate comments.

"Hey Jordan, I didn't recognize you with that scruff on your face. Did your razor brake?" Jenn adds.

Jordan chuckles and responds, "Haha, I change my look a lot. Sometimes I do the clean shaven look and sometimes I don't. Sometimes I spike my hair and other times I just throw a cap on. It's all about how I feel, not to mention that I get bored quick."

"That's what I was just saying to Principal Kate. We can't get too comfortable and we constantly need to shake things up in life. Right Kate?" Jenn responds and smirks.

Jenn looking around the park mumbles, "So, where's the rest of the Marvel Crew? Thor, Widow, Iron Man... they got to be around here somewhere."

Kate hears her low mumble and tries to keep a straight face.

"I'm sorry Ms. Jenn, I didn't hear you... Did you ask me something?" Jordan questions.

"No, no, honey... I just asked if you came alone or did you already make friends at the school and come down with them?" Jenn quickly covers her tracks.

"I'm alone and just came after a workout to chill out and take in some sun. I'm heading back now. See you both later tonight at the dance?"

"Yes, see you later Jordan." Kate replies.

"Bye, see you at the dance." Jenn replies.

Jordan walks back to his towel and puts his shirt back on. Then packs up and starts walking out to leave the park.

Kate turns to Jenn with a serious tone, "OK, this is actually the first time that I wish I had Nurse Madison's job instead of mine." Kate carries on....

"I would be like... Jordan, come to my office

I have to take your temperature and give you a shot, the flu is going around."

"Jordan, turn your head and cough I have to check for a hernia."

This time Jenn bursts out with laughter, "Haha, that was good Kate."

CHAPTER FOUR

◆ ◆ ◆

Jordan returns back to his dorm and does a few errands. He gets some clothes ready for the Annual Student Kick-Off Dance tonight. He decides to lay down and wants to take a nap before tonight's welcoming event.

Jenn and Kate are still in the park as they continue to talk and joke around.

"Kate, WTF? He didn't look like that yesterday during his orientation with me."

"He had more clothes on yesterday, Jenn." Kate replies sarcastically but joking.

"No really Kate, today he looked like he was our age and not a student. It must be that not shaving thing. It gave him that bad boy type of edge…. didn't it?" Jenn replies.

Kate remains composed, "Either way, shaven or not, he's naturally good looking."

"Kate! Are you kidding? He's fucking hot! I want to slap that ass until my hand falls off!" Jenn responds.

"He's only 18, actually 19 on Monday, and he is one of our students." Kate says in a professional manner.

"C'mon Kate, this is me you're talking to... You can't fool me. I know how your mind works and I bet you're having some interesting thoughts right now."

Kate responds, "OK, I can't lie, my mind is definitely playing some images. It's that kink curse I told you about."

Jenn tries to reason, "Kate think about this. You and I have gone to several of these spanking clubs, events, and munches together right?"

"Yeah of course, Jenn... so?"

"We see a good number of younger people at these events. Some are 18, 19, 20, 21... whatever. I can remember not too long ago at that spanking club in Springfield when you took that young guy behind the curtain with your leather strap in hand. Remember?"

Kate smirks, "Oh, he was a total bad boy

and he got it good!" They both laugh and Kate continues, "Yes, of course I remember, but that was a spanking club and we talked first. He wanted it and I was more than happy to give it to him."

Jenn reasons more, "And how about the time I spanked that young boyfriend and girlfriend couple in the main room in front of everyone? Remember that? They were probably 18 or 19 also."

Kate smiles and jokes, "I do, that was fun to watch."

"...but, it's not...the.." Kate tries to further explain but Jenn cuts her off.

"Kate, listen to yourself. As long as they are 18, they are legal and they can attend. So my point is... if we met Jordan at one of those events it would be the same thing. We would be so into spanking him and you know it. You would at least be interested in talking to him and comparing interests."

Kate thinks for a moment then responds, "If I met him at a fetish event and he looked like that, I would never think he was 18 soon to be 19."

Jenn carries on, "Exactly! That's my point. Think of the rope events we've gone to and the spanking clubs where we've played scenes with younger, as well as, older people. It's the vibe that matters, not their age. I know you would definitely be interested in finding out what his kinks are. Shit, so would I! I would be all into finding out more about him and the things that turn his crank if he was ever at those fetish clubs."

"Yeah, but it's different because he would be there willingly, so we would already know that he's into it." Kate reasons back.

"Well, you're right about that, but hey you never know. I just hope he misbehaves and gives me a reason to take him to Discipline Hall. Now that would be an adrenaline rush…. stripping him down to his birthday suit and seeing that body… all of it! Oh, don't worry, I would sell you a ticket to watch." Jenn smirks and slightly laughs.

Laughing again, "Like I said my friend, you are in rare form today. I think we should stop at the pharmacy and get you a fresh pack of AA batteries. I have a feeling you'll be needing them tonight after the dance. Hell, maybe you'll use them as soon at you get home from here." Kate smirks back.

Jenn reacts, "I told you I was crazy and horny knowing I'm without kids and a husband this weekend. I may need your help… a play date."

"Gladly, Missy! I'll be keeping my eye on you tonight. Now lets go home I need a nap before the dance." Kate responds.

"I agree a nap is in order.... And, no need to stop for AA batteries. I have a brand new toy that's rechargeable!" Jenn adds.

CHAPTER FIVE

◆ ◆ ◆

Friday night arrives and the annual student kick-off dance is just getting underway. This high end event serves as a meet and greet reception and takes place in the Recreation Center. There's a band playing with a DJ spinning songs between breaks. Amazing food is prepared and drinks are served as well.

Since the legal drinking age in Connecticut is 21, there will be no alcohol served to those underage. It will be served to only those students wearing a wristband with verifying IDs that meet the legal age requirement.

The founders Ms. Marilyn and Ms. Marj are standing at the front entrance as people start to arrive. Principal Kate, Ms. Jenn, Nurse Madison and all the faculty are there also walking around to greet everyone and monitoring everything.

Special event security has been hired to assist with the normal ground security for the school tonight. Since the school policy has a maximum of 40 students per semester only about a quarter of them will be new first year students. The school generally maintains a pretty even ratio of boys to girls. Tonight each student is allowed to bring up to 4 guests and/or family members to the event.

Kate, Jenn, and Madison are together talking as Kate reminds them to check and monitor wristbands for the alcohol station and also when they are walking around.

"Remember guys, if someone with a valid wristband gets someone else a drink that isn't legal, we have to step in. We have to be aware of the entire room and not just where the bartenders are." Kate explains.

They both agree and Madison walks away to look and starts canvasing the recreation center. Jenn smiles and compliments her best friend, "Kate, you look stunning as usual tonight. That dress, those shoes, good God girl!"

"Awe thank you Hun, but I was just about to tell you how insane you look in that dress. You are rocking that look! Red looks amazing on you!" Kate smirks and responds.

"I couldn't decide between this dress and my police uniform but I chose the dress and packed the uniform. It's in the car in case I need it for later." Jenn smirks back.

"I see you're still in rare form, huh? Well, you won't need it, cause I might be the one to arrest you later tonight. So take that, Officer Jenn!" Kate replies.

The recreation center fills up fast with students, their friends, and their families. The 10 or so new students begin to mingle and introduce themselves to each other. The 30 or so returning students share their experience and offer guidance. They make themselves available for any questions the first year students may have.

It's a close knit school with a great vibe thanks mostly to the founders Ms. Marilyn and Ms. Marj, however, they are always quick to give proper credit to Principal Kate for the way she's been running the school since she took over. They truly feel Kate is running The Academy just as good, if not better, than when they ran it.

Some of the new students really stood out to the staff this week specifically Alyssa, Hunter, and Jordan. Jordan especially has made quite an impression on Principal Kate, as well as, Ms. Jenn. He can't help but notice how hot Principal Kate looks tonight as it's obvious that she also made quite an impression on him as well.

Everything about her really gets his blood flowing. From her amazing physique to her black belt status and martial arts background. He also loved the way she carried herself during their orientation. It really drew him in as he reflects again on how the conversation was flowing effortlessly between the two of them. The young athlete starts to get these thoughts and fantasies once again as he's standing around sipping his ice tea and taking it all in. There's just something about her that brings out every fiber in his body & mind.

Principal Kate rocked his world yesterday during their orientation. She set him spinning with desire and he's been re-playing it ever since. That stern tone she used really sent him over the edge as he did his best and tried not to show it. His mind starts to recall how one minute she would be so nurturing, calling him sweetie and darling, yet like a light switch she would turn on her strict mode. This sarcastic flip-flopping of her voice turned him on beyond belief. Inside he was totally hot thinking about her aggressively handling and spanking him. His erection yesterday during orientation was bigger than the state of Texas where Kate went to college. Tonight he's doing all he could not to get an uncomfortable hard on at this event.

The party is now in full swing inside the

recreation center and students are having a blast. Most students are dancing while others are just hanging out and talking. The women faculty continue to walk around and monitor everything.

Jordan isn't shy as he starts making new friends. Of course most of them are female. Then in a flash a cute, petite student that has a killer physique and an adorable, bubble butt grabs his arm and pulls him on the floor to dance.

He has no idea that her eyes locked onto him yesterday when Principal Kate was walking him around and taking him on the school tour. Needless to say, this young cutie wasted no time when she saw Jordan standing there and now they're dancing up a storm.

After a few songs they decide to get off the dance floor and head for an area less noisy to talk. She flashes him a beautiful smile and introduces herself.

"Hey I'm Julia." She says as her eyes opened widely.

The two instantly hit it off. Julia went on to mention that she's about to start her second year at the school and how she absolutely loves it. They talk for at least 20 minutes and then quickly pull out their phones texting each other their cell numbers. Then they both start dancing together again.

Julia immediately felt an attraction to Jordan with his spiky, surfer type, dark blonde hair and big green eyes. She took in all of his physique from his nicely sculpted arms to his wide V-shape that tapered into a small waist. He had the type of body type that she finds incredibly attractive. Actually, he has the body any girl would find attractive including the faculty. It's the kind of physique that is sexy and muscular but very proportionate. It's not overly freaky looking like those steroid guys in the hardcore bodybuilding magazines with veins popping out of their eyeballs.

It was obvious that Jordan was in amazing shape. Julia managed to steal some glimpses of his legs and round ass as they were dancing. She was now extremely interested and was feeling a bit turned on by the sexy new student. After a few more dances they got off the floor and continued their conversation. It didn't take long and just as quick as Julia met Jordan two other girls came over and quickly made their presence known. The two girls introduced themselves to Jordan. One girl was named Amy, and the other was Cassidy, who goes by Cassie. They are both starting their 3rd year at the school.

Julia manages to be friendly with both girls but kind of has an issue with Cassie, the stunning brunette. Julia isn't really fond of Cassie since last

103

year when she came close to punching her out. She suddenly had a flashback of that day and how Principal Kate stepped in and quickly defused the situation. Right in that moment Julia's mind flashed to images when Principal Kate held her over her curvy hip and delivered slap after slap to her cheeks. It's accurate to say that Julia did more dancing that day over Principal's Kate hip then she did tonight with Jordan at this kick-off dance party. So it's very obvious that Julia still resents Cassie from the looks she just gave her. It seems everything about the pretty brunette is still a sore spot for Julia and it really gets her heated.

Principal Kate is standing by and just watching this all unfold. She notices Julia was a little taken back and maybe even jealous that they pulled Jordan on the dance floor while she was talking to him. The beautiful principal walks over to comfort Julia. She approaches her with open arms for a loving hug.

"Hi sweetheart, just wanted to say hello. I think you need a big hug." Principal Kate then embraces her.

"Hey Principal Kate, Ya' I really needed that. Thank you Ma'am." Julia responds.

Principal Kate did her best to offer Julia some loving advice and comfort her using her motherly instincts. She looked over at Amy and Cassie dancing with Jordan. Then she turned to

Julia and said, "I know you probably think he's smoking hot and granted he is..."

This got an immediate giggle out of Julia hearing that come out of Principal Kate's mouth. The two of them continue to have a "just between us girls" type of conversation that starts to help Julia calm down.

"You still have to remember honey, he's only 18 and this is his first year. I saw the way he looked at you and I think he's really interested. It's normal for Jordan to mingle and make as many friends as possible at this party. You know what it felt like being the new kid at school here during your first year." She offered in a sweet caring tone.

Once again, this put Julia more at ease as she exhaled and said, "Thank you Ma'am. You're awesome, and I really respect and appreciate you. We are all lucky to have you as our principal." This melted Kate's heart as she smiled and muttered, "Awe". Then she hugged Julia again even tighter re-assuring her.

"So, did you get his number?" She asked the young student.

Julia replied, "Ya, he sent it to me via text."

"Well, I suggest calling him later tonight or early in the morning and asking him to workout with you. You can also skip the workout and take him for a hike or swim tomorrow. Maybe pack a lunch and go to the Falls. Sound cool?" Principal Kate suggests.

"OMG, I will.. Totally... That's an amazing idea! Thanks again Ma'am." Julia replied with a big smile. Principal Kate now takes the opportunity to remind Julia not to lose her cool tonight regarding Cassie.

"Remember last year honey? Do not get yourself worked up and overheated like that again." Principal Kate says in a nurturing but semi-stern tone.

Julia again immediately reflects back to that specific day when Principal Kate took her into Ms. Marilyn's house and really tanned her cheeks. Those images were now prominent and playing over and over filling her mind. She quickly remembered the embarrassment she had when Principal Kate aggressively yanked her shorts down and corrected her behavior right in front of Ms. Marilyn.

Principal Kate simply giving Julia that quick reminder helped. Julia was now totally engulfed and vividly recalling all those memories in her mind. She was now feeling a little jittery inside as she often does whenever she thinks back to that day of her first spanking.

She then looked straight at Principal Kate and said, "Oh, God yes Ma'am. I will never forget that spanking you gave me. You sizzled my ass. It was on fire for a couple of days." Then she quickly caught herself.

"Oooops, sorry didn't mean to swear Ma'am."

Principle Kate gave her a cute little smirk and replied, "It's OK that wasn't a bad swear darling. You should hear the words that come flying out of my mouth after a couple of glasses of wine with my girlfriends. Just don't make it habit or swear in front of teachers." Julia instantly laughed out loud with images of her Principal swearing up a storm from a wine buzz.

"Like I said, you're the best principal ever! We are all lucky to have you." Julia stated.

Principal Kate then makes another suggestion that comes to her mind. She reminds Julia that preventative spankings can be very helpful just as the handbook states. The women faculty always remind students of this choice. It is especially beneficial to those that are on the verge of slacking off or misbehaving. The staff is quick to point out that a PM level 5 hand spanking may be just the thing needed for them to avoid further misbehaving and getting a level 7, 8 or worse with the reform strap.

Principal Kate now standing face to face with Julia lifts her chin up so they have total eye contact and once again reminds her.

"You know sweetheart, a trip over my lap for a PM spanking might help you get this jealousy out. It seems you are a lot like me, and it doesn't take much to get you overheated. You just need to learn how to manage it better. OK? Think about it, I'm here all night and it might be just what you need to start the school year off right."

Julia looks straight into Principal Kate's eyes but doesn't say a word. It's obvious that she knows her principal is right. Her feisty temper often gets her in trouble. The truth is, she did a lot of soul searching and learned a great deal about herself after Principal Kate spanked her that day.

Principal Kate then chimes in, "Oh, and I promise you Julia, a PM spanking won't be as hard as the spanking you got from me last year. In fact, I don't even have to be the one to give it you. We can ask Nurse Madison or Ms. Jenn to give it to you."

Julia replies and admits, "I know you are right Ma'am. I realized a lot about myself ever since you spanked me. I was never spanked before so it was eye opening. I know I'm still a bit over-heated right now and Cassie has a way of getting to me."

Principal Kate then takes the initiative and motions for Ms. Jenn to come over.

CHAPTER SIX

◆ ◆ ◆

Ms. Jenn responds to Kate's hand motion and starts to walk over to them. The pretty brunette is built very similar to Kate. She has a lean, curvy figure with beautiful hips that lead down to full, strong legs. Her nicely toned arms are also an eye-catching feature and a result of her weight training sessions with Kate. They definitely go at it hard in the gym and it shows. Julia's now feeling a little anxious and nervous as she watches Ms. Jenn walk over to them.

Kate explains, "Hey Jenn, Julia here may need a PM spanking tonight. I suggested that maybe you or Nurse Madison give it to her if she agrees. She just told me that I'm the only one that has ever spanked her. So, it may be helpful if she gets a spanking from someone else."

Ms. Jenn turns to Julia with her nurturing voice, "Is this so sweetie? What for?"

Julia responds, "I tend to get really jealous and Cassie has a way of just setting me off." As she points to the 2 girls still dancing with Jordan.

"Jordan and I were talking and they kind of came over and just swooped him away!" Julia replies in a feisty, heated tone.

"Well, I personally think a little heat on your tush will take away some of the heat your head is feeling. We'll kind of redirect it… ya' know?" Ms. Jenn responds jokingly.

Ms. Jenn's comment makes both Julia and Principal Kate crack up.

Principle Kate laughingly replies, "Oh Jenn, you are a piece of work my friend. Stay and talk to Julia for a while. I'll be around to check in. Julia either way with Ms. Jenn or me you'll be in good hands. Hands that really care about you."

Principle Kate then walks away leaving the student and teacher to further talk. As she walks by the dance floor Amy and Cassie pull her to dance with them and Jordan.

"C'mon Principle Kate, dance with us." Amy yells out.

Kate smiling joins in for part of the song

with them. More students and even some teachers were already on the floor. Kate was trying her best not to cast too many looks in Jordan's direction. She quickly turned and danced with Nurse Madison who was also dancing in a group of teachers & students having fun. She then finished dancing to the song and decided to go to the bar for some water. She notices the smell of marijuana coming from a group of 3 students. There's 1 boy, Cade, a brand new student standing and talking to 2 girls, Alyssa and Nicole. Alyssa was also a brand new student and Nicole was starting her fourth and final year.

She confronts them all immediately with a commanding voice, "You 3, I want to see you outside in the hallway right now!"

She then looks over to Nurse Madison on the dance floor and signals for her to come over. When Madison arrives Kate says, "Maddy, can you help me for a minute?"

She then takes Nurse Madison with her to confront the 3 students in the hallway. They absolutely smelled like pot. Principal Kate reads them the riot act right there in the hallway. She was especially upset with Nicole since she is now a senior, going on her last year.

"Marijuana, vaping, smoking in any way is not allowed on this campus. You all signed the handbook and you're all aware of the rules. Nikki,

I'm really surprised at you." Kate continues. "Is it just pot? Cause if we find narcotics of any kind you are all out of here.. Period!"

Nikki spoke up with a tremble in her voice, "Yes Ma'am, it's just pot. We smoked a couple joints behind the dorms. I had them and shared."

"Very well, that's all I needed to hear. Let's Go… Follow me… All of you."

"Maddy come with us, I could use you." Kate blurts out.

"Absolutely!" Nurse Madison replies.

Kate then hastily walks out of the re-creation center and heads straight for Discipline Hall with Cade, Alyssa, and Nicole. Nurse Madison had new student Cade by the arm as the 2 other girls walked willingly with their heads down. The group instantly had looks being thrown at them from every direction. The students that were in the hallway and those outside, knew exactly where the five of them were marching to.

Ms. Jenn and Julia were sitting outside at a picnic table and talking just like Kate asked. Both of their heads also turn as the group marches by. Principle Kate looks their way and calls out, "This is why a preventative spanking works, Julia. They will be getting a lot more than a level 5 hand spanking." She continues walking them toward Discipline Hall.

In that moment Ms. Jenn gently rubs Julia's upper back showing her a very nurturing side as they continue their conversation. Principal Kate arrives with the 3 students and Nurse Madison at the steps of Discipline Hall. She clicks a button on her key chain that unlocks the door and then she holds it open.

"Let's go.. Inside!" She calls out to them. Once everyone was inside she clicked her remote again and locked the door. She then locked the inside deadbolt to ensure no one would be entering.

"Maddy take Alyssa and Nicole to the main room and wait for me."

"Cade.. Lets go... March Mister!" She orders, grabs him by his arm, and walks with a purpose to room 2.

Upon entering the room she lets go of him and locks the door behind her. She then immediately grabs the school wooden paddle from the implement closet. The young first year student backs up as she walks closer toward him.

"So, this is how you want to start your first year at my school young man?"

"If you want out of my school and the consent form, now is the time to say so."

Cade shakes his head no as fear takes over him. He's frozen in place as Principal Kate marches toward him with the paddle in her hand. She stands face to face with the young student and with a pointed finger she scolds, "I'm gonna redden your hiney for smoking pot at my school!"

She then grabs the belt on Cade's jeans and gives it a hard tug causing it to unbuckle. She wastes no time and quickly unfastens the top button of his jeans. Cade's natural reaction to move his hands over the top button is met with a resounding <SLAP> across the back of his left hand.

"Don't you even think about it!" The stern principal warns as he quickly pulls his hand away saying, "Oow" and shakes it vigorously from the sting of her slap.

Principal Kate then places her hands inside the waist of his jeans. She makes sure to also grab the waist band of his underwear as well. Then she gives a quick, forceful yank that makes both pieces of clothing fall together, straight down to his ankles. Cade naturally puts his hands over his dick as he feels embarrassed and tries to cover up.

"I've seen it all before sweetheart!" Principal Kate says in a stern, sarcastic tone as she yanks his hands away and looks right at his dick. She grabs one of his arms and pushes him over the padded bench. His cute rear end is now bent over and prominently in her vision. She raises the wooden paddle and forcefully goes to town. <CRACK, SMACK, CRACK, CRACK> She lands a flurry of hard swats across his cheeks that instantly solicit a response.

"YEOOOW...OOOW!"

The sound of his voice along with the paddle connecting on his bottom echoes all throughout Discipline Hall. Nurse Madison who is holding the 2 girls in the main room hear every nuance.

<SMACK, SMACK, CRACK, SMACK> Principle Kate meant business as she delivers four in row across his ass. He's trying not to cry as a few tears start forming in his eyes.

"OOOOWwww.. OOOH.. OUCH" Are the words flying out of his mouth.

He naturally starts to squirm and he raises his torso off the bench prompting Principle Kate to yell, "BEND OVER!

Get Back In Place.. Fanny Out Cade!" As she pushes him forcefully back in place over the bench.

She then adds pressure on him by pushing him down with the force of her left arm on the small of his back. She delivers a flurry of at least another 4 swats that has Cade completely bawling out.

He did his best to stay in place but he couldn't help that his legs were shaking and trembling from the spanking he was getting. Principal Kate was now holding Cade even tighter. She proceeded to deliver her final 5 swats with the paddle as Cade clenched his butt cheeks in anticipation. <CRACK, SMACK, SMACK, CRACK, SMACK> Landed hard across his totally red bruised bottom.

"Stay bent over and don't even think about moving until I come back!" She scolds and then walks out the door and into the main room carrying the paddle in her hand.

CHAPTER SEVEN

◆ ◆ ◆

Nurse Madison is there holding Alyssa and Nicole. She instructs Alyssa, the first year student to move away and stand against the mirrored wall. Nurse Madison lets go of her arm and Alyssa moves quickly and stands exactly were Principal Kate told her to. She has the look of complete fear in her eyes, kind of like a deer caught in headlights type of look. She stands silently and watches as Principle Kate is face to face with Nicole. Nurse Madison stands directly behind Nicole and now places her hands on both of Nikki's biceps.

"I'm extremely disappointed in you Nikki." Principal Kate scolds. "You're a senior... in your last year. You know better than this." Kate scolds while moving a high padded stool in the center of the room.

Nicole with her jet black hair and dark eyes said nothing. She couldn't raise her head as she kept looking down at the floor. Kate looked over at Nurse Madison standing behind the girl and holding her arms.

"Maddy, you know what to do." Nurse Madison without hesitation lifted Nikki's red, baby doll dress up over her hips and yanked her thong undies down to her ankles.

"NO... Please.. Please." Nikki cried out.

"Do either of you want out of the school.. The consent form?" Principal Kate asked. They both quickly responded in unison, "No Ma'am."

Nurse Madison knew from experience exactly how Kate wanted Nicole positioned on the high padded stool. She pulled Nikki over the stool forcing the student to bend over. She then stood in front of her and pulled Nikki's dress up high, all the way to her shoulders. She held it up while resting her arms on the top of Nicole's shoulders.

"PERFECT Maddy!" Principle Kate commented to her peer.

Nicole was bent over with her slightly chubby, cute bare bottom facing out to Principle Kate. With no further time wasted, and as Nurse Madison held her in place, the strong principle swung the paddle with a vengeance. <CRACK>...

Echoed loudly off the walls. All it took was for that one swat to connect and Nikki lets out a resounding cry, "OOOWWW!"

The tears quickly pour down her face. She immediately dances from leg to leg as Principal Kate delivers another 4 in a row to her bare bottom. <CRACK, SMACK, CRACK, CRACK> Nikki couldn't hold still. She twisted and turned from feeling the sting of the paddle. She was actually hopping up and bouncing as she desperately tried to wiggle her cheeks to calm the pain.

"WAS IT WORTH IT HONEY?" Principle Kate yelled in a strict tone.

Nurse Madison now reaches down and grabs Nikki's hips to move her back in place over the stool. The students ass is already bright red in color.

"Got her Maddy?" Kate asks her friend.

"C'mon Nicole, keep your fanny out." Nurse Madison coaches.

Nurse Madison now positions Nicole back in place over the stool. She confirms with Kate, "Got her!" Then she holds her down with a little more pressure.

Principal Kate then places her left hand on the small of Nicole's back and delivers 7 in a row pausing only slightly to grab the girls hips and move her back in place. Nicole couldn't help it.

She continued to wiggle and bounce up from the pain.

Her cries echoed off every wall. When she would open her eyes to let the tears out, she would see herself in every mirror from every angle. Alyssa was already crying from just watching Nikki getting paddled. She was scared shitless of how that paddle was going to feel on her ass. Principal Kate moved in closer to Nicole and now wrapped her left arm around her waist. Nurse Madison was still holding her in place as well. Kate gave a firm tug and Nikki's hiney popped out a little farther. She didn't waste another minute.

<CRACK, SMACK, CRACK>…. "KEEP THAT FANNY OUT NICOLE!"

<CRACK, SMACK, SMACK>…"C'mon stick it out for me!" The stern Principal reprimanded. She had a tight hold on Nicole and now pulled her over her left hip.

"Hold her down, Maddy." She instructed sternly. Nurse Madison pressed her weight on Nikki's shoulders and Principal Kate held the crying student over her hip. She glued her eyes onto Nicole's red cheeks without ever looking anywhere else. She then raised her arm high and gave her one last flurry with the wooden paddle. She delivered at least 4 with enough force that would make anyone cry. Nicole's ass was complete toast as she continued to cry out.

"OK Maddy, let her go." Principal Kate signaled to her nurse. Nurse Madison escorted Nikki who was crying profusely, right next to Alyssa. Alyssa now trembling with fear knowing she was next, feels Nurse Madison grab her arm and march her in place over the stool. Alyssa is an 18 year old, olive skinned beauty with light brown hair and matching eyes. She looks so cute tonight in her athletic top and tight designer leggings.

Nurse Madison then puts Alyssa in the exact same position bent over the stool. Once again, she leans over the front of the student. She then places her arms resting on Alyssa's shoulders to keep her in position.

Principal Kate is standing behind Alyssa bent over the stool. She calls out, "Time to reveal those cheeks honey!" Then forcefully grabs the waistband of her leggings and with one hasty tug yanks them down exposing a tight athletic ass.

Alyssa was shaking and looking at her bare ass from every angle in the mirror. <CRACK>... Suddenly, she lets out a loud scream, "YOOO-OOWWW." Principal Kate landed a hard swat with the wooden paddle that connected square across her cheeks.

Madison again tightens her grip and applies more of her weight on Alyssa's shoulders. She then gave Kate the nod who wasted no time and delivered 5 in a row. <CRACK, CRACK, CRACK, CRACK, SMACK> The room was now filled with loud cries from the new student.

Alyssa repeated the same pattern as Nicole by bouncing up and down in pain and dancing from leg to leg. Principal Kate grabs her cheeks with force and pulls her back into place. She continues to squeeze Alyssa's ass until she has her in the exact place she wants her. With Nurse Madison still holding her tight she puts her left arm around Alyssa's waist and pulls her upward and slightly over her left hip. Then just like with Nicole, Principal Kate swung that paddle with a vengeance delivering at least 6 in row.

She held Alyssa with expert force as the young girl was kicking and squirming over her hip. Principal Kate didn't hesitate at all. She just squeezed even tighter around her waist. She placed her right leg over Alyssa's legs to prevent her from kicking her legs high and squirming too much. She now had them locked in place.

It was obvious Kate knew how to give a spanking and maintain control. With Alyssa crying like crazy and Nurse Madison holding her shoulders, Kate finishes with 5 merciless swats. <SMACK, CRACK, SMACK, SMACK, SMACK>

She then calls out, "OK, let her up Maddy." Nurse Madison did so and marched the crying student right next to her friend.

Principal Kate warns Alyssa sternly, "If this ever happens again, I will totally strip you down to your birthday suit and use the reform strap on you. Is that understood?"

Alyssa immediately answers while still crying, "Yes Ma'am."

"As for you Nicole, your getting 3 right now with the reform strap. You should've known better.. Maddy get the strap out of the closet." Principal Kate then grabs Nicole and puts her up against the mirrored wall.

She spins her around and scolds, "Face in.. Fanny OUT!" She grabs her dress and pulls it up as she stands on Nikki's right side. She grabs her arm and tightly holds her in place. Nurse Madison stands behind Nikki slightly to the left with the reform strap.

"Deliver it Maddy." Principal Kate instructs.

"Put that hiney out for me Nicole!" Nurse Madison instructs Nicole.
"Farther.. Farther."

Principal Kate moves her hand under Nicole's belly and pushes it out farther. This put her cheeks exactly were Nurse Madison wanted them. With a solid swing and a swish sound thru the air, Nurse Madison delivered the reform strap across

Nikki's bare ass. <SMACK>

Nikki once again bawled out as principal Kate kept her tight grip forcing her butt to stay arched outward. Nurse Madison who is probably the most nurturing of all the staff was also in full stern mode and disappointed at the senior.

"This is exactly what Zero Tolerance, No Nonsense means NICOLE!" She scolded as she aggressively landed another with the reform strap on Nikki's already bruised cheeks. <CRACK>

Nicole crying loudly, had a natural reaction and tried tucking her body and moving inwards. That didn't work at all since Principal Kate was right there to push it back out. <CRACK> Nurse Madison delivered the 3rd and final spank with the strap.

"Thank you Maddy." Principal Kate complimented and then let go of Nikki who once again had tears flowing.

"Both of you get dressed and go straight to your dorms. Do not go back to the dance. Your night is over. Oh, and you are both grounded tomorrow!" Principal Kate ordered.

"Come follow me Maddy, lets check on Cade."

❖ ❖ ❖

The 2 women walked together into the room that Cade was still in. He was basically in the same place leaning over the spanking bench. Principal Kate now with Nurse Madison by her side pulled a padded low stool to the center of the room. She spun Cade around as once again he naturally tried to cover his dick.

This made Nurse Madison joke and say, "Why do these boys even do that? Do they really think we haven't seen it all before?" Principle Kate just chuckled and again slapped his hands away making him quickly expose his privates.

"Maddy, finish him off with a good old fashion hand spanking over your knee." She ordered.

Nurse Madison sat on the padded stool and tapped on her lap, "Let's go Cade." Cade still had his jeans and underwear pulled down to his ankles causing him to waddle over slowly. He then placed himself over her lap.

Nurse Madison adjusted her leg, and forcefully grabbed his ass giving it a slight lift, "That's right... fanny up darling." She grabbed and held onto Cade's cheeks and lifted them even higher. She then raised her right hand high over her head and started delivering a good old fashion hand spanking just as Principal Kate ordered her to give him. The sounds of her hand stinging his rear end echoed loudly.

"Perfect, my friend. Cade you are in good hands." Principal Kate chuckled.

"Go directly to your dorm after she spanks you. And by the way, you're grounded tomorrow!" The principal adds as she turns and starts to walk out of Discipline Hall. With every step she takes her ears are filled with the sound of Nurse Madison's hands lighting up Cade's cheeks.

She's just about out the door and still hears the slaps along with Cade's voice echoing, "owww... oooh.. uhh... ouch."

"MMMMmmm. Music to my ears." She says to herself out loud as she exits the building.

CHAPTER EIGHT

◆ ◆ ◆

Principal Kate went back to the dance and continued to monitor the event. Outside Ms. Jenn was still talking with and comforting Julia as her phone was getting a few text messages. Ms. Jenn suggested Julia look at her phone as they paused their conversation. There were several messages from Jordan concerned and asking how she was. He mentioned in his text that he quickly got off the floor after just 1 dance with Cassie and Amy to find her and continue talking. He also mentioned how he was really connecting with her and even went looking for her to make sure she was OK. Most of all, he wanted to know where she was and if she was coming back to the dance.

Julia responded with complete honesty telling him that she was really into him and that she got overheated regarding Cassie rudely pulling him away. He totally understood and put her at ease by letting her know that he was equally into her. In fact, his text to her read.... I'M REALLY, REALLY INTO YOU. He also mentioned how absolutely stunning she looked in her dress, which again helped her further calm down. Several compliments went back and forth between them. Jordan also let her know that Cassie isn't his type and that she totally is.

Julia took Principal Kate's advice and asked Jordan to go out with her tomorrow to Kentville Falls. Jordan's response back was... ABSOLUTELY! I'll call you in the morning... Julia's next text back to him stated she was tired and was calling it a night. She was still a bit upset and didn't want to go back and have Cassie set her off. Jordan's final text of the night to her read.... I totally understand. I can't wait to see and get to know you more tomorrow. You are stunningly beautiful inside and out ☺!

Julia then shared these text messages with Ms. Jenn as she started walking back to her dorm. The two of them walked arm in arm more like good friends instead of teacher/student. Ms. Jenn made sure to express once again how proud she was with her for just chilling out and not getting into trouble.

Julia smiled back at her and shockingly replied, "Ms. Jenn, Can you give me a good spanking? I feel like I really need it. I need to cry and let it out." This took Ms. Jenn by surprise but she responded with her witty humor to help lighten Julia's mood.

"Well, it's your fanny sweetheart."

It worked as Julia let out a cute chuckle. The two of them went inside her dorm. Ms. Jenn immediately suggested they sit down and talk first. They sat face to face and had a very open conversation. She reinforced how proud she was that Julia caught herself getting mad but managed to settle down. She asked Julia to explain her feelings and wanted to be absolutely sure about her decision to get a good spanking from her.

Julia replied trying her best to make sense of what she was feeling.

"I've learned a lot about myself over this last year Ms. Jenn. Especially, after Principal Kate spanked me." She went on.

"I realized that I always try to hold in my emotions, I just hold everything in. Then I get so overheated and over stressed with everything I want to pop. I truly believe that getting spanked is something that can help keep me grounded and relieve a lot of this stress and anger." Julia expresses clearly.

Ms. Jenn couldn't help but be impressed by

Julia's soul searching and the way she spoke her truth. She simply listened as the young student went on.

"I've done a good amount of reading and I've studied a lot about human behavior. I finally understand why some people voluntarily hurt themselves. Some are cutters and others are smokers or drinkers. I've come to terms with my personality type. I need accountability and structure. I've never had it growing up. Does that make any sense Ms. Jenn?"

Ms. Jenn in a very comforting tone holds Julia's hand and replies, "It makes more sense than you even know honey. I see it all the time. That was also me at your age. Actually, it still is me to some degree, but that's another story that we can talk about some other time. We're here to focus on you."

She continues, "Go ahead and do your nighttime routine and get into your pajamas. I'm going to ground you for the rest of the night. You are not allowed to go back to the dance.

Come back out here to the living room when you are ready."

Julia listens and heads into the bathroom to clean up and then into her bedroom. She puts her pajamas on and within a few minutes she returns to the living room. Ms. Jenn takes a moment and explains that she is going to take her over her lap and will be administering a spanking with her hand. She also lets her know that she will be checking in on her often during the spanking. Ms. Jenn pulls an arm-less kitchen chair into the living room and confirms.

"OK honey, you mentioned that you want this to be a good spanking... Correct?" She watches Julia shake her head yes.

"It won't be as hard as Principal Kate gave you for fighting that day but I will absolutely give you a good spanking. Your cheeks will be nice and red when I'm done but I doubt that you will have any marks or evidence. I know you may be going swimming with Jordan tomorrow, so it shouldn't be noticeable." Ms. Jenn adds.

Julia looks down at Ms. Jenn sitting and acknowledges, "Thanks Ms. Jenn, I know that I really need this."

Ms. Jenn mentions, "Now some people will cry and some won't. This is a PM spanking and it's all about you. You have to make sure it accomplishes your goal. Don't be afraid to let it out. It's not just about the pain, and sometimes it's just about crying to relieve the stress. Trust me, I know this from experience."

Ms. Jenn lifts her dress enough to uncover her bare legs with just a peak of her panties. She taps on them and says, "OK, come over honey." Julia does so and positions herself over Ms. Jenn's lap. She then feels her teachers fingers slide inside the elastic waist of her pajamas. Ms. Jenn lightly touches her fanny and says, "Lift a bit, Hun." She then pulls Julia's pajamas down to her knees and exposes her bare bottom. She raises her hand and starts to immediately warm her cute cheeks up.

<slap, slap, slap> She delivers a few medium slaps to Julia's bare bottom... <slap, slap, slap>... Alternating from left cheek to right.

Julia manages to hold her emotions in aside from a slight, "aaah", "uuuh", "ouch".

Ms. Jenn softly scolds by saying, "This is for your own good darling." <slap, slap, slap> She slightly increases the force of her slaps. <Slap, Slap, Slap>.

"Is this what you need sweetheart? A good spanking on your cute rear end from time to time?" She asks.

Julia is now beginning to feel it and reacts with a shake in her voice, "Yes, Ma'am."

Ms. Jenn in a nurturing manner replies, "Well sweetheart, you can ask me to spank you anytime. I'll be glad to put you over my knee whenever you need it." <Slap, Slap, Slap, Slap>

Julia's cheeks now have a nice red glow as Ms. Jenn continues to alternate and evenly distribute her hand slaps across Julia's rear end. She starts to hear Julia whimper into what sounds like it could be the beginning of a cry.

"Good girl... that's it.. let it out sweetie." She's says to Julia as she spanks a little harder with her pretty hand. <Slap, SLap, SLap, SLap>

Feeling totally overcome with stress and needing to release it, Julia finally starts to form tears and responds a little louder, "Ooooow... OOwww".

Ms. Jenn gives her a few more hard, stinging, slaps. <SLAp, SLAp, SLAp> Julia now really responds, "OOOOW.. UUUUhhh". Ms. Jenn pauses for a moment and places her hand on Julia's bare cheeks to feel the heat of them. She takes a good look and confirms that each cheek is totally red in an even manner.

"Stand up my dear, turn around, and let me see." She tells her.

Julia does so as she is slightly crying and starting to get the release she needs. Ms. Jenn monitors and takes another look at her red bottom as she checks in with her. She looks at her face and pays very close attention to her student. She mentions to Julia that this is her call. She can stop or continue if she feels she needs more.

Julia looks at Ms. Jenn and makes her decision, "It's OK Ms. Jenn, I need to be spanked harder.

I need to really cry and get it out."

Ms. Jenn agrees with a nod and takes Julia's hand escorting her back over her lap and into position. This time she raises her right hand high over her head and delivers four much harder, more intense stinging slaps.

<SLAP, SLAP, SLAP, SLAP> These hard slaps work and now Julia goes into a full much needed cry. She does all she can to stay in place and not clench her cheeks as Ms. Jenn delivers a few more even harder. <SLAP, SLAP, SLAP, SLAP, SLAP> Julia, holding on to Ms. Jenn's ankles, squirms and presses herself deeper into Ms. Jenn's legs but maintains her position thru the hard slaps.

Ms. Jenn comments, "I'm impressed honey. I know I'm spanking you hard. You must have a super high tolerance because you're not even clenching those cheeks or squirming all that much." Then she continues to deliver another 4 hard slaps.

<SLAP, SLAP, SLAP, SLAP> Julia feels these harder, intense slaps and now really responds with a louder cry, "OOOW... OOOO.. OOW". She starts squirming more over Ms. Jenn's lap. She is doing all she can not to clench her butt.

Ms. Jenn stops for a moment to monitor and looks at Julia's cheeks as she has her over her lap. She notices a bright shade of red on them and softly pats them as she checks in with her student.

"Just checking on you honey. I know you are crying so hopefully this is accomplishing what you want." She mentions.

Julia sobbing replies, "It is and I'm forcing myself to stay in place. I'm trying not to squirm too much or clench. It's taking everything I have not to."

Ms. Jenn lightens the mood with her humor, "Well, I can honestly say that you are one tough cookie! I might start calling you iron cheeks."

Julia manages a pause in her crying to give a slight giggle.

Ms. Jenn shares, "I've been spanked in this position during our faculty training sessions. Last time Principal Kate was my partner and demonstrated a hold to go along with this position over her lap. It wasn't as hard as I'm spanking you, and I was still dancing and squirming all over her lap. So like I said, I'm impressed with you, little miss iron cheeks."

Julia ass is now on fire as she feels Ms. Jenn's hands monitoring, touching, and pressing her cheeks. She doesn't say anything but gives an indication that her rear-end is tender with a few sounds, "ooo....ouch... ummm". She wiggles and presses herself further into her teachers legs.

Ms. Jenn again comments, "Yep, I'm impressed Julia. Even the big, strong boys I spank can't hold still like this. They squirm like crazy."

Julia replies, "I'm embarrassed enough about being bare over your lap, but I'm kinda insecure about the way my butt looks when I clench."

Ms. Jenn pauses for a moment to take in what Julia just said then responds,

"You are beautiful inside and out. Try not to be so hard on yourself."

Julia responds, "Thank you Ma'am…. I'm learning….trying."

"My door is always open and you can feel free to come and talk to me about anything…. And I mean anything." She tells her in a motherly type of tone.

Julia replies, "Thanks Ms. Jenn, I absolutely will… I promise. I'm really hard on myself and I need to change that."

Ms. Jenn counters, "Well, let's take the first step to change that right now."

She catches Julia completely off guard and quickly delivers four extremely hard slaps <SLAP, SLAP, SLAP, SLAP>.

This absolutely forces Julia to all out squirm and clench her cheeks. She starts crying again and this time the tears are rapidly falling.

Ms. Jenn now stops and takes a moment as Julia's laying over her lap to address her insecurity comment.

"There… you clenched and I saw it. You're still beautiful, darling."

"I imagine it's those little dimples, maybe a little bit of cellulite that you're referring to?" Julia sobbing, shakes her head yes.

"Well, we all have it and it's something many of us struggle with. Even those very fit and in shape have it. Trust me, I know all about it. You don't want to see mine when I clench my butt." She says as she pulls Julia up.

Once again she takes a moment to check in on her and monitor the spanking that she gave. She turns her around and looks closely at her bottom. This time she can absolutely see the red marks of her hand prints.

Julia now has the tears steadily coming down her face. The extra intensity of Ms. Jenn's slaps gave her exactly what she needed. Ms. Jenn asks her if this worked and accomplished what she needed. Julia continues to cry and let it all out as she agrees that the spanking can stop. She definitely got the release she needed.

Ms. Jenn now stands up and gives her a warm hug. She then reaches down and pulls Julia's pajamas back over her butt with care, realizing the tenderness she must have.

The two of them sit back down to talk. Ms. Jenn continues to give as much positive reassurance as possible to Julia. She feels like Julia finally had a breakthrough.

She makes one additional comment to her, "Remember honey, you are at a time where your hormones are going crazy right now. Talk to me, talk to Principal Kate, or Nurse Madison. It's normal to have so many unsettled feelings." She then pulls a tube of Arnica cream out of her purse.

"Let's rub some of this on. It will help soothe your skin and hopefully you won't have any marks for tomorrow."

She then leads Julia onto her couch and instructs her to lie flat on her tummy. She lowers her pajamas one last time and softly rubs a good amount of the cream onto her glowing, red cheeks. She then pulls the pajamas back up, gives her one last hug and one final check.

"Are you OK honey? Do you need to talk about anything else?"

Julia responds, "Thank you Ms. Jenn, this was exactly what I needed. Despite a tender hiney, I actually feel a lot better and much more calm. The spanking worked for sure, but the way you cared and talked to me was a major part of it. So again, thank you." Julia stands up, gives her teacher a tear filled smile, and a big hug.

Ms. Jenn warmly replies, "You're welcome, sweetheart. You were absolutely right and it seems like you needed this. I'm impressed with how in tune you are with yourself. Remember, you can come and talk to me anytime about any-thing." She then walks out of her dorm room and ends her time with Julia.

Julia now retreats into her bedroom and turns off the lights. Her mind is so much clearer as she absolutely got the release she needed. She feels like a huge weight is now lifted off her shoul-ders. She relaxes and relishes in the moment and this feeling of clarity and calmness. Ms. Jenn was right and she is now fully aware and in touch with her body, her mind, everything that gets her mad, and also everything that turns her on. She realizes how much she learned about her sexuality ever since that first spanking from Principal Kate. Now it's all coming together and making perfect sense to her. She's been diving into everything from kinky books and pictures, to fetish websites, to spanking videos, and even some porn.

Laying there in bed she starts to get that familiar jittery feeling that she's become aware of. She reaches down and starts touching her pussy and immediately notices how wet it is. She closes her eyes as numerous kinky thoughts fill her head. The wetness in her pussy further intensifies as she continues to engage her mind as her fingers deeply explore.

She is totally turned on thinking about the spanking she just received from Ms. Jenn. She reflects on how she absolutely loved the caring mom side of her, and the way she was so understanding and nurturing.

She pushes her fingers deeper and side to side, thinking about how she loved it even more when Ms. Jenn didn't hesitate to get really stern and slap her harder. She realizes how she was at the brink of climaxing all over Ms. Jenn's lap, especially when she was embarrassed and couldn't refrain from clenching her cheeks. She is now totally aware that being vulnerable and embarrassed, in addition to being spanked, is a huge turn on for her. Totally turned on she reaches into her nightstand and grabs her vibrator. She softly inserts it into her soaking, wet pussy and just lets herself go.

Again, she replays that feeling of being so vulnerable over Ms. Jenn's lap a few short minutes ago. She fantasizes about Principal Kate and the first spanking she ever received. Even though it hurts like hell she loves how her cheeks feel when a firm hand slaps them. Despite her insecurities, she actually loves having her butt on display and having people look at it. She even enjoys looking at it herself and gets turned on seeing red marks on it. After months of soul searching and learning about her body, the importance of that mind-set connection, she now totally understands it and can even explain it. She knows that she is a full on exhibitionist that loves to be vulnerable, spanked, and controlled.

She's come to the realization that her feisty personality is one that needs to be man handled even woman handled. She knows that she needs to be held accountable and she absolutely loves being put in her place.

A new image now enters her mind as she's intensely playing with herself. Her thoughts shift and focus on Jordan and all his hotness. She now creates a movie in her mind of him totally dominating her. She wonders if he's into it as her hormones kick into overdrive. She works the vibrator all over her pussy and clit to these kinky thoughts as she shakes and climaxes. Feeling beyond amazing, she lets out a loud and pleasure filled, sexy moan.

This was her final release for a rollercoaster of a night. Finally, she's relieved and this orgasm has left her in a restful state. She closes her eyes and quickly drifts off to sleep.

CHAPTER NINE

◆ ◆ ◆

Ms. Jenn now returns back to the Kick-Off Dance as it's winding down to a close. There's about 30 minutes left before it's over. Everything looks good as she resumes monitoring and sends smiles to her peers that are also walking around.

Principal Kate is talking to some parents along with Ms. Marilyn. It was another great event despite the infractions of Alyssa, Cade, and Nicole. Student behavior overall was excellent as the staff now waits for the DJ to spin his last few songs.

It was another great event despite the infractions of Alyssa, Cade, and Nicole. Student behavior overall was excellent as the staff now waits for the DJ to spin his last few songs. The dance comes to an end and everyone has left the recreation center. The cleaning crew comes in as the faculty says goodbye to each other and looks forward to the start of school on Monday.

Principal Kate and Ms. Jenn walk out together and head for the parking lot. They walk across the beautiful lawn that's landscaped to perfection, shadowed with accent lights. It's a warm, comfortable summer night, the kind that makes you want to stay outside and just take it in. Kate and Jenn make small talk over the dance event as Kate then properly thanks her for comforting Julia.

"Jenn, thank you for taking the time to talk with Julia. She is a feisty one and it's important for her to take a moment, talk things out, and decompress. I'm the same way so I recognize and know that personality type first hand. I saw how she calmed down as you listened and comforted her... you're amazing!"

"You're welcome, I know it helps to have someone just listen as you vent. She's a good student that has grown a lot over the last year. She's very in touch with her mind and body." Jenn responds.

Kate asks, "Did she ask you for a spanking? I know she was contemplating getting one."

"She sure did. I gave it to her in her dorm room. It was over my knee with my hand, but definitely harder than the usual PM type spanking. She wanted to get that release and cry so it took a while. I checked in with her several times and she let me know every step of the way. I'm really impressed with her maturity and the way she held herself accountable. Kate, she's really grown a lot since last year and she credits you. So as far as amazing goes… it's you my friend. The students are lucky to have you." Ms. Jenn compliments.

"Thanks Jenn, their lucky to have all of us in this environment. Julia's a good girl and I really like her. She babysits for Josh sometimes and he enjoys when she comes over and watches him." Kate replies.

"Just so you know, I gave her a hard spanking that left some hand prints on her cheeks. Hopefully this helps her stay focused and not lose her cool. Afterwards, we talked more and I applied some Arnica cream to her. She's going out with Jordan tomorrow either swimming or hiking, so I didn't want to leave evidence of the spanking she got." Jenn informs her.

Kate then turns to her friend, "Perfect, that is just what she needed. Speaking of spankings…. How are you doing, my beautiful friend? Still wound up or did you calm down?"

"Calm? Are you kidding? I have such an adrenaline rush right now from just giving a spanking. You know that feeling that happens from the whole power dynamic. It's hard not to get that rush when I just had a cute set of cheeks squirming all over my lap.

Plus, I'm kid-less and hubby-less this weekend! I need a play date!" Jenn replies.

"In that case, I know just what you need Jennifer. Now, in your car and follow me…. We're going straight to my house, Missy!" Kate says with authority.

"Yes Ma'am." Jenn smirks back.

Kate gets in her car and watches as Jenn followers her orders. She pulls out of the parking lot on route to her house and checks her rear view mirror. Jenn is following just as directed. Kate starts to get that tingly feeling in anticipation of their late night play session that's about to go down. She reaches down and discreetly makes a call on her phone while driving.

"Hey, it's me… It's on tonight, everything's perfect and going as planned. We're on our way to my house. Everything still good on your end?"

She continues, "Awesome! I can't wait to pull this off and surprise my friend. She's stunningly beautiful with a creative and kinky mind to match. Tonight she's really gonna be blown away."

Kate then hangs up the phone and smiles

to herself as she slips her right hand under her pretty dress and begins to rub her pussy. She feels the wetness accumulate on her panties as she continues to gently rub herself on her drive home. Knowing that she's getting carried away, she then pauses from playing with herself in order to avoid having an orgasm right there while driving home. She looks back in her rear view mirror and thru the darkness, gives a covered smile at Jenn. Her mind is now overflowing with vivid images on how the late night session is about to unfold.

"Mmm, my beautiful friend, I'm about to totally blow your mind!" She says out loud in her empty car.

The Academy series continues with book 3 of the story "Play Date". What's in store for Ms. Jenn and Principal Kate along with rest of the female staff?

What students may need to be marched into Discipline Hall. What kinky adventures may unfold? What secrets may get revealed?

Come onto campus and experience all the action, kinky, and erotic events that are about to happen at The Academy.

The Academy
Play Date
Book 3

◆ ◆ ◆

CHAPTER ONE

◆ ◆ ◆

It's Friday, just about 11:30pm and The Annual Student Kick-Off Dance at The Academy just wrapped up. It was another very successful event that served as a meet and greet for students attending the prestigious, private boarding college. Principal Kate, as well as, the entire female faculty were in attendance to socialize and also monitor the dance party. Overall student behavior was excellent tonight, despite one incident that the stern principal quickly dealt with about an hour ago. As Kate's driving home her thoughts are totally focused elsewhere. This late night drive home is silent yet quite eventful to say the least and so far, Kate has used this solitude to her advantage. She's been engaging her mind and planning exactly how she wants this late night play session to go. A few minutes ago, as her BMW was hugging the dark, quaint, back roads of Connecticut, her fingers couldn't help but travel under her pretty green dress and plunge into her moist pussy. It's been building all day and her mind is already connected to her body, as she squirms with elation of just how good her own fingers are feeling right now.

Before she goes too far and loses all self control, she makes the decision to pull her fingers from her pussy and to stop playing with herself. She knows it's best to delay the orgasm that she was about to have right then and there while driving home. Instead, she knows from experience that it's going to keep building and elevating within her and tonight when it's the right time, it's gonna be one epic climax!

Her eyes keep checking her rear view mirror as now her fingers are tapping the steering wheel with nervous energy. Her mouth is watering in anticipation of all that she may soon be tasting. Kate is wet beyond belief and so turned on as she keeps creating this vivid, kinky, movie over and over in her mind. She's clearly picturing tonight's scenario with many of the details on how everything will play out downstairs in her "kink room", the room that she cleverly disguises as a huge exercise room.

She double checks the rear view mirror again to make sure her beautiful friend and peer

Jenn is still following. These were the direct orders she gave her a few short minutes ago. So far, Jenn is following Kate's orders to a "T" as she's driving her own vehicle and following close behind her. Kate can only assume that Jenn is also fantasizing about their little escape, especially, since she came right out and told her how much she desperately needed this play date.

She made it clear to Kate today over lunch, just as she has time and time again, that it's a vital part of who she is as a woman. Jenn stressed that she craves this escape from her routine, vanilla sex life and her non-stop duties of being a mom to 3 kids. The two women have become the best of friends and they've worked together at The Academy for the last year and a half ever since Principal Kate hired her. Jenn is such a great fit for the unique school. The students, as well as, the faculty just adore her. She's a dedicated professional that brings her caring and nurturing maternal instincts along with her to work every day. However, just like the rest of the staff, she is also a strong no nonsense disciplinarian when she needs to be.

There's no denying that Kate and Jenn have so much in common. They are similar in so many ways that it's comical and they joke about it all the time. This may be the very reason why the bond and friendship they share is so special.

They are both loving moms that always put their families first. They're extremely driven, dedicated fitness buffs, that have pretty much the same personality and the same overall outlook on life. They do so much together from working out, to shopping, to even going to fetish clubs and kinky events. They both thrive on creativity and can easily get bored if their minds aren't challenged often. On a professional level, they both totally understand and embrace the power they have from being in a position of authority at their jobs.

Kate and Jenn are both emotionally and physically strong women that firmly believe in using spankings to correct misbehavior. They are more than fair and very understanding when it comes to minor student infractions, however, they absolutely operate on the zero tolerance approach that the school is known for. They totally understand and often experience the adrenaline rush that comes from administering bare bottom spankings and being in this position of such power.

They are fully aware and in-touch with their sexuality and the kinks that get their wheels turning. They both appreciate having each other to share this special "kinky" bond with, and thru their in-depth conversations, they realize how similar they are in this area as well.

Both of them put a major emphasis on the mind/body connection and how it enhances everything, especially everything sexual. So it's no coincidence that they focus on engaging the mind before anything physical ever happens. They are both very erotic and uninhibited when it comes to sex, so anything that is not vanilla, routine, or boring always seems to resonate with both of them. They love using toys, dressing up, role-playing, using rope, blindfolds, and they are definitely into spanking…. all forms of it… giving and getting. They totally enjoy "switching" and disciplining each other, and they never hesitate to hold each other accountable, which results in filling their needs in that area.

To this day, Kate is the only person that Jenn has confided in regarding when she cheated on her husband. Of course, Kate tries to help and she does all she can to try an ease her friends guilt about it. She reminds Jenn that is wasn't really an "affair" so to speak, since it was just one night of reckless abandonment with a guy that totally dominated her. She had a specific fantasy that was consuming her and when she couldn't fight it any longer, she made it a reality and experienced it with a Dom. When the two of them became the best of friends, she easily opened up and confided this to Kate. That conversation was the catalyst for Kate to also share her deepest and darkest kink secrets. That was the start of how these two women established this special and kinky bond they share today.

So Kate, being similar to Jenn, pretty much knows that she is having kinky thoughts in her car as she's driving. Once again, Kate's intuition is spot on and 100 percent accurate as Jenn is doing all this and more!

As she's driving her car and following Kate, her mind is also creating vivid images of all that is soon to unfold. She then takes her right hand off the steering wheel and slips her fingers under her beautiful, red dress and begins to play with herself.

She starts to lightly rub her pussy as she thinks about Kate's quaint country house with the kink room downstairs. She's been waiting for the right time to play and experience many of things they've talk about. She knows Kate is a true friend but she also views her as a mentor. It was her that really helped wake up the sexuality and all the creativity that Jenn has inside. Kate was also the one that introduced her to several fetish websites, kink events, and spanking clubs. Jenn gives all the credit in this area to Kate and often thanks her for being instrumental in trying to help "spice things up" with her vanilla marriage.

They've spent so much time with each other and they always seem to have a blast.

They've gone out shopping together for sex toys, clothing, costumes, and anything that would help inspire creativity in the bedroom. Unfortunately, to Jenn's frustration, it just didn't work. She came to the realization that it just isn't a part of her husband's world. Also, she was very honest with Kate when she told her that even if her husband was into it, she doubts that he would be the one to fulfill her fantasies. Sadly, she just doesn't view him in that manner.

Kate, totally understood this and had already experienced this same thing prior to her divorce. Since she's a mom herself, Kate was able to relate the guilt she had when she took the lead role in ending her marriage. Above all else, she's been such a valuable friend, that is always quick to lend an ear, or give Jenn a shoulder to cry on.

Even though both of them have gone to several fetish events and spanking clubs, they manage to keep their kink relationship in check. They have no problem talking about everything sexual and they always enjoy sharing ideas. However, up until now their play has been limited to just spankings and holding each other accountable.

So needless to say, with all this build-up and having the Student Kick-Off Dance behind them, they didn't hesitate to seize the moment and embrace this "play date". They both are pretty wound up after giving some serious spankings to misbehaving students tonight. It's the whole mind/body connection, coupled with the power exchange, and the dynamic of having that kind of authority. True kinksters know this is one of those things that really get your blood pumping!

As for Ms. Jenn, well she's been horny all day. Her creative mind was hyped right from early morning. That's when her husband took their 3 kids away for the weekend to Vermont to visit his parents. There was no way she wanted to waste the opportunity to play if it came up. She's been craving and needing an escape from her vanilla sex life to fully explore her creativity and fantasies. That was even before she had to administer a preventative maintenance spanking tonight to Julia, a 2nd year student, that is quick to get overheated. She took the time and talked to Julia, calming her down at the student dance. tonight. The feisty student was at the verge of losing her cool with another fellow student named Cassie, who she's had past issues with.

Cassie's a third year student that seems to get under Julia's skin quite easily. Julia is well aware of the friction between them and how Cassie can just get to her. Julia explained to Ms. Jenn that she has indeed grown a lot since last year when Principle Kate gave her an intense bare bottom spanking right in front of founder Ms. Marilyn. This was the result of her instigating a fight with Cassie over work chores.

During their conversation, Julia expressed very clearly to Ms. Jenn that she needs to be spanked and held accountable for her actions. Ms. Jenn was more than happy to oblige when the cute student came right out and asked her for a spanking tonight.

So just about 30 minutes ago in Julia's dorm room, is when Jenn finished giving a stern, bare bottom spanking to the feisty student. She's still feeling the adrenaline rush of spanking Julia as her cute hiney was squirming, clenching, and pressing into her legs from the fierce sting that her hand was delivering. She took her time administering this bare bottom spanking and made sure that it gave Julia the result she needed and requested.

Prior to that and earlier today, she spent the afternoon with Kate and together they both enjoyed their last Friday off for a while, since the school semester gets started on Monday. It was a beautiful 80 degree September day, so they packed their lunch and took in some sun and the sights at Kentville Falls State Park. They both locked their eyes on what they called a delicious snack coming out of the water with a body like a Greek God and a face that was equally enticing. Jenn was really fired up and she was lost in thought trying to decide if she wanted to kiss, bite, finger, or spank his perfect ass. She settled on all the above and even added some more items to that list. Then being the good friend that she is, she offered to sell Kate a ticket to watch that event! So yes, Jenn's mind has been on a kink roller coaster all day, twisting and turning at top speed.

When Kate and Jenn found out that the hot guy at the park was Jordan, a first year student, that turns 19 on Monday, they were simply enamored. They both met him the previous day, the final day of orientation. Each one of them spent a good amount of time talking and getting to know him. However, today at the park he looked completely different to them. Kate's sarcastic response to Jenn on why he looked so different today was simple and priceless…. It was because he had less clothes on!

Principle Kate was already wrestling with her own feelings from yesterday during her orientation with Jordan. These were feelings that she hasn't felt in a long, long time and feelings that she never felt with a student. She found herself constantly struggling to keep her mind on the orientation. The fact is, she was completely drawn into his whole vibe. This wasn't even reasonable and she kept reminding herself over and over… Snap the fuck out of this Kensington! I'm 34, why am I so infatuated with this 19 year old guy?

She wondered why she talked in more detail about spankings with him than anyone she could ever remember. Even the people Jenn and her have met at the fetish clubs and events don't initially talk in this much detail. There seemed to be a complete openness about Jordan that she gravitated to. Their conversation flowed effortlessly over one of her favorite subjects, which was spanking of course, and she was intrigued as to why this was.

Jordan didn't seem to be affected at all with the details she shared and everything she showed him. He completely maintained his composure and remained collected when she took him thru Discipline Hall and gave him the complete tour. This is usually not the case and most students react with some intimidation when the stern principal takes them on the school tour and shows them the inside of that building. Especially, when she warns them and makes it clear that she will have no hesitation in yanking down their pants and administering a serious spanking to their bare bottom if they misbehave. Most of time she just gives them a quick glimpse of the several discipline rooms and the variety of benches and padded tables in those rooms.

The thing that usually gets the most impact is showing the students the school reform strap and how it can be used on them in the main room with its large mirrors on every wall. Principal Kate always explains that it's important for someone to see themselves getting spanked because being vulnerable and embarrassed is a huge part of correcting behavior. She always goes on to mention how the research shows this is a major reason to the success of bare bottom spankings as a method of discipline.

So again, this is usually just a quick mention as most students show some sort of fear in their eyes. In fact, many of the students will never even step foot near Discipline Hall during their four years at the school. For some reason Principal Kate didn't get a sense that Jordan had any of this common fear that she's seen before in students. She was actually impressed that he maintained his composure and just took it all in. He even gave Principal Kate several solid reasons and excellent feedback on why corporal punishment works as a method of discipline.

So that was all it took as Kate's mind has already been in overdrive since yesterday. Plus, her mom is taking care of Joshua, her 9 year old son and most prized possession. She knew that the timing was right and that she has complete freedom and an empty house for the entire weekend.

Kate is also revved up with events from the student dance tonight. She and Nurse Madison had to march three students into Discipline Hall for smoking pot. She didn't hesitate to correct the behavior of two girls, Alyssa and Nicole, and one boy Cade. She adamantly administered the wooden paddle to their bare cheeks until they were dancing up a storm. In addition to this punishment, she also instructed Nurse Madison to use the reform school strap on Nicole, as she held the senior student in place for instigating the whole charade. It was clear that being a senior and already knowing the protocol for misbehavior like that would warrant extra discipline. After they both left her crying a river they went back to deal with Cade, a freshman, who's cheeks Principal Kate already paddled red.

She felt it necessary to send a strong statement to this young man before his school year even started. Especially, since freshman boys have the habit of getting in the most trouble at the school. Therefore, she further orchestrated the pretty school nurse to take Cade over her lap for a good old fashion hand spanking. She watched in delight as his round cheeks squirmed in pain over Madison's lap. She knew that he was really feeling the sting of her hand much more now, since his cheeks were very tender from the paddling she gave him.

So it wasn't hard to understand why Kate was totally turned on right now as further evidence from the moisture in her panties. The stern principal is never one to be without creativity or some type of scenario flowing thru her kinky mind. She totally understands and embraces her sexuality and all it entails. She also knows that once her kinky, creative mind is wound up, it's going to be hard to stop until an orgasm happens. That in combination of her gorgeous friend being in need of a serious play date and release, is all that her mind is focused on right now.

CHAPTER TWO

◆ ◆ ◆

Within five minutes of her house Kate gives one final glance in her rear view mirror to make sure Jenn is still following. She flashes her trademark smile in the darkness as she confirms that her orders are being followed perfectly. She reaches and presses a button on her car's digital screen and makes a phone call.

"Hey, we are just about at my house... How long for you? OK, perfect.. I'll already be downstairs getting into it with her. Make sure you stay as quiet as possible and lock the door after you come in. Change into the outfits we planned and come downstairs. Awesome, sounds good babe... See ya' soon."

She then pulls into the driveway of her

quaint country house and within a few seconds watches as Jenn does the same. They both get out of their cars and smile at each other with a ton of excitement, as well as, a ton of nervous energy. Jenn opens her trunk and takes her gym bag out.

Kate shoots her a smirk, "Got everything you need in there, Hun?"

"Absolutely!" Jenn flashes her a sexy look.

"Nervous?" Kate asks.

"Absolutely!" Jenn replies.

They both laugh in their cute familiar way and Kate takes her friend's hand and leads her into the house. Once they are inside, she closes the door and gives Jenn a big warm, hug. It immediately makes Jenn release a small amount of the nervous energy, but more importantly, it totally makes her feel safe and welcome. Again, she takes Jenn's hand and starts to walk her downstairs to her kink room, disguised as an "exercise" room.

They go inside the large room together and Kate immediately adjusts the lights. She makes it romantic and dark yet still bright enough to see their reflections on all of the mirrored walls. She lights a bunch of candles and turns the music on so it's just loud enough to be audible, yet not get in the way of any dialogue.

"I'm going to freshen up and I'll be back

down. You can do the same in the bathroom down here. When you're done, come right back into this room and stand in that corner." Kate points then continues.

"I want you to face inwards with your eyes closed... Got it?" She commands Jenn.

Jenn quickly replies, "Yes Ma'am."

They walk out of the room together as Jenn goes her way to freshen up and Kate walks upstairs.

Jenn takes a moment to clean up and excitedly gets herself together. She grabs her gym bag and returns to the kink room taking a moment to reflect and just to enjoy the moment... Every aspect of it... From the past conversations they've had, to the flirting all day today, to the evening spanking events from the student dance. She enters the room and is immediately lost in the aroma, as well as, how beautiful the candles look reflecting on the mirrors from every wall. The soft music is just enough to entice her mind and add to the mood, but she knows the real ear candy is everything that Kate will be orchestrating and commanding. The dialog is a huge part of the turn on for both of them, as well as, just about every kinkster on the planet.

Jenn takes one last look at herself from every angle of every mirror on the walls of the room. She's still in the red evening dress from to-night's event that just about everyone under the sun complimented her on. She walks to the exact corner Kate had pointed her in and takes one last look with her eyes wide open. She inhales and takes in a nice deep breath, then closes her eyes as instructed.

CHAPTER THREE

❖ ❖ ❖

K ate takes a few extra minutes to freshen up upstairs as she puts on a killer outfit. She visualizes the scene and reconnects her mind to the scenario that's in her head. She's totally engulfed in thought and now she's ready to get it all started.

She walks down to her kink room and sees that Jenn is exactly where she ordered her to be. She takes a moment without saying anything to just look at the rear view of her stunningly gorgeous friend. There she is, standing in the corner with that insane red dress on. She first takes in her thick, brown hair that flows down to beautifully toned shoulders. She then looks at her strong, yet still feminine arms. Her eyes then shift downward and take in the view of her curvy hips that lead down to her amazing ass. Last but not least, she stares at her legs and just how perfect they look. Her thighs are full and strong looking as they taper down to her defined calf muscles. She also can't help to appreciate the killer shoes she has on! Kate is totally into it as her eyes scan the entire room. She loves what she sees as she catches Jenn from every angle.

Kate's mind is there and she's completely turned on as the adrenaline rushes into her body. Her kinky exercise room has big, thick mats on the floor, but she still calls out to Jenn to let her know she's about to come into the room. She wants Jenn to focus on her senses, so she makes sure that her eyes are still closed. Plus, she doesn't want her to catch one glimpse of the outfit or the way she looks right now.

"Eye's closed Jennifer?" She asks.

Jenn responds, "Yes Ma'am."

Kate then enters her kinky mirrored room and goes straight to unlock the closet at the far end. She also unlocks her storage trunk, grabs a few things, and starts to approach Jenn. Even though Jenn's eyes are closed tightly, she can totally sense that Kate is moving toward her and possibly within an arm's reach away. Somehow, she just knows it…. She senses her, smells her, and can even feel her without a single touch.

Kate approaches silently, and is careful to

not make noise as she walks ever so lightly. She lets each step gently sink into the matted floor. The music plays low in the background and helps to conceal any overall room noise that isn't up-close dialogue. Kate is now standing on the left side of her pretty friend. She leans in and waves her hand in front of Jenn's face to make sure her eyes are fully closed. Then, without saying a word, Kate takes her right hand and grabs a small amount of Jenn's gorgeous thick brown hair. She quickly wraps it around her fist and gives it little tug. This makes her sexy friend tilt her head back and immediately open her mouth with a response, "Mmmm... uuh."

To play it safe, Kate also places her left hand over Jenn's eyes. She gives her hair another little tug as once again she reminds her in a stern voice, "Keep those eye's closed Jennifer!"

Jenn tilts her head back again and responds thru clenched teeth, "uuhh... Yes Ma'am."

Kate now places her mouth fully over Jenn's left ear and gives a slight exhale letting her breath float and penetrate down Jenn's ear canal.

Jenn reacts with another moan, "MMM-mmm."

With her mouth fully engulfing Jenn's left ear, Kate whispers but in a very stern tone…..“Tonight, you are no-one's mother… tonight you are no-one's wife… you are no-one's teacher… Tonight, you are the sexy and absolutely stunning woman that my eyes are admiring…. Tonight, I'm not your Principal.. I'm not your best friend.. Tonight, we are not at school. This means we can swear all we want. There's no need to use all those professional or old fashion words like we have to at The Academy. I want you to be as vocal and as free as you want to be. I don't want to hear the words vagina, private parts, bottom, or rear-end. I want to hear pussy, ass, tits, and any other nasty word that you want to say. Got it Jennifer?”

Jenn responds with a slightly heavy breath, “Yes Ma'am.”

Kate now releases Jenn's hair wrapped around her hand and places a blindfold over Jenn's eyes. She walks around her pretty friend, letting her fingers trace along Jenn's shoulders. She stands on her right side and resumes the same position with her mouth over her right ear. Jenn, with her arms down at her side, can't help but feel a part of Kate's bare leg pressing against her right hand. Her mind immediately pictures Kate in a sexy lingerie as she feels the wetness form in her pussy. At the same time she feels Kate's mouth over her right ear and she can't help but let out a soft moan, “mmmm.”

Kate questions, "You OK, Jennifer?"

"Yes Ma'am! I'm more than OK… I'm fucking turned-on!" Jenn says with zero hesitation.

Kate continues her stern whisper, "Tonight the rules are… You must be absolutely clear and tell me when you're getting close to having an orgasm… Your safe word is RED…. Say RED and everything stops immediately, and we check in…. Use Yellow and I'll proceed slowly, knowing that you are not far from saying RED. Is that clear Jennifer?"

"Yes Ma'am." Jenn replies as her pussy is accumulating more wetness.

Kate once again grabs a handful of Jenn's hair and leads her in the center of the kink room. Kate glances in the mirror and loves the image she sees. She's totally into it as she sees herself using just the right amount of force to escort Jenn into the middle of the room.

Kate releases the TRX hanging cable straps from the ceiling and then walks behind Jenn. She reaches out and holds onto the cable hanging down to her right. She calls out, "Right arm up… grab it."

Jenn listens and Kate helps guide her to grab onto the handle as her right arm is now over her head.

Kate now walks around to the other side of her and repeats the process, "Left arm up... grab it."

Jenn follows directions and now she's standing with both of her arms extended upwards over her head and holding on to the cables extending from the ceiling. Kate positions her mouth right back over Jenn's left ear.

"Do you have any idea what I'm about to do to you?" She asks.

Jenn replies, "You're going to spank me, Ma'am."

"Excuse me?" Kate questions.

"You're gonna redden the fuck out of my ass!" Jenn replies louder.

Kate walks behind her and gives a lift to her beautiful, red dress pulling it up over her curvy hips. She takes her time making sure it's securely going to stay in place. She resumes her position in Jenn's ear and replies, "That's not all I'm going to do you, Jennifer. I'm going to totally devour you!"

She walks behind Jenn and squats down so her eyes and mouth are now level with her amazing ass. It looks absolutely adorable with the full bottom part of it peeking out of her white laced undies. Kate takes both of her hands and forcefully grabs the right cheek of Jenn's ass. She holds it tight and sinks her teeth right below the fleshiest part that's sticking out underneath the panties. She gives it a sexy, little bite and leaves her mouth on it as she sucks a small piece of Jenn's right cheek through her teeth. After a few seconds she lets her bite subside and lets her tongue explore the little red mark she just made.

Jenn responds, "ouch" then "mmmm." She was totally caught off guard expecting to feel a hard spank when instead she felt Kate's sexy bite that had just enough force to give her a little jolt. With the blindfold on she can't see or even predict Kate's next move. She doesn't care, all she knows it that she loves the feeling of being vulnerable, and that's the way she's feeling right now. Not to mention, she finds Kate so damn sexy!

Jenn begins to breath harder as she feels Kate's tongue explore her ass. Kate now lifts the right side of the lace panties all the way up into a thong and traces her tongue all over that side of Jenn's ass. She continues to give it a soft, full lick as she totally flattens out her tongue, gliding it all over Jenn's womanly ass from top to bottom. She then stands up, walks around, and stands face to face with her beautiful blindfolded friend.

Jenn's breathing grows harder as she feels Kate's lips aren't far from her face. Without any warning, Kate once again reaches back and gives a little tug on Jenn's hair immediately forcing her to open her mouth and yielding the response, "ooo... mmm."

"Tongue out!" Kate sternly commands her.

Jenn listens and sticks her tongue out as far as she can. Kate then eases up the grip of her hair but still leaves her right hand holding onto the back of Jenn's neck. Kate takes a moment and glances in the mirror. She wants to remember this image... She needs to remember this image... It's fucking hot!

She takes her tongue and gently touches Jenn's. Jenn responds with approving and sexy moans, coupled with some very deep breaths. Kate loves hearing this response and further intensifies their kiss. She moves both of her hands around each side of Jenn's neck and cradles it. She continues to let her tongue explore every inch of Jenn's beautiful mouth. Kate's tongue softly glides over Jenn's pearly white teeth, then back out and over to taste her full lips. She takes a moment to gently suck, then nibble, then again gently suck on Jenn's full bottom lip.

She commands Jenn once again, "Tongue out for me, Jennifer."

Jenn listens and once again sticks her tongue completely out. Kate places her bottom lip on Jenn's tongue and gently moves it side to side and back and forth. Jenn navigates her tongue all around to taste Kate's full lips and follows thru by also sucking and nibbling on them. Kate now begins to breathe deep and she lets out a sexy, "Mmmm."

After a few seconds she pulls away to purposely tease her blindfolded friend. She walks back around her and once again squats down to be eye level with Jenn's ass. She lets a minute or two go by keeping Jenn in suspense waiting for the next thing to happen. Jenn remains blindfolded with her arms extended over her head and still holding onto the high cable grips.

It's totally working and the suspense is driving Jenn crazy. Her mind is flooded with images of Kate doing all kinds of things. She still has no idea how Kate looks tonight but her mind has already created some insanely, sexy pictures in anticipation. She thinks to herself that Kate must look "killer" in some sexy outfit. She already knows that her legs are exposed since she felt them brushing against her hand a few minutes ago. Jenn continues to let her mind lead the way as she visualizes their scene.

She can't wait until Kate takes this blindfold off of her. She knows it will be amazing to see their reflection in the large mirrors as all this action goes down.

Her panties are now fully wet as she stands

there vulnerable. She has no idea what Kate's next move is and she totally loves that feeling!

CHAPTER FOUR

◆ ◆ ◆

Kate remains behind Jenn and at eye level with her ass. She gets really turned on looking at it like this; so up close and right in front of her face. After a few minutes of getting her fill and keeping Jenn in suspense, Kate gracefully shifts from squatting to kneeling, as she starts softly kissing Jenn's left ankle. She proceeds and slowly licks all the way up the inside of her left leg. Kate makes sure to take her time and thoroughly taste every inch that she's licking. She lets her tongue travel slowly above Jenn's knee, then she pauses for a moment to build suspense, and then continues licking all the way up to the inside of her inner thigh. Again, she pauses for a few moments and pulls her tongue completely off Jenn's skin. The tension has Jenn so turned on she's going crazy with anticipation. Kate then reconnects her tongue on Jenn's inner thigh and lets it travel as her licks get closer and closer to Jenn's pussy.

Jenn lets out a sexy, "Mmmmmm…"

Kate lets her tongue gently grace the outer and inner labia that's peeking out of Jenn's lace panties. She reaches out and pulls the left side of Jenn's panties over and up making it into a complete thong. Kate then gives another sexy bite, this time a little harder, on Jenn's left ass cheek.

Jenn immediately responds, "Ouch."

Once again, Kate follows the little bite up with a kiss, then starts to suck and lick all over the red teeth marks she just made. Jenn's response quickly changes, "Mmmm."

Kate then stands up and remains directly behind her. She glides her hands up and down Jenn's arms that are still extended over her head. She alternates soft touches with firm squeezes as she questions….. "Have you been a good girl, Jennifer?"

"No Ma'am, I've been bad." Jenn confesses.

Kate replies, "How bad, Jennifer?"

"I've been really FUCKING bad, Ma'am!" Jenn lets out.

"Well, you know exactly what I do to bad girls!" Kate's stern voice echoes.

Jenn is wet with anticipation as her pussy is tingling in harmony with her entire body. She's loves the feeling of vulnerability along with everything else she feels when Kate strips her down and gives her a serious spanking. Without saying another word, Kate reaches down and aggressively yanks Jenn's underwear down to her ankles exposing her beautiful ass. She moves to Jenn's left side, and uses one of her favorite, signature spanking positions. Kate shifts her weight and firmly pulls Jenn in place over her curvy left hip.

Jenn knows this position well, however, tonight it feels even more intense since she can feel the skin of Kate's bare leg as her body is held in place. Kate wraps her left arm around and under Jenn's waist. She gives a firm lift that makes Jenn's ass arch out farther. Kate tightens this hold on her left arm as it's wrapped around and under Jenn's waist, but she also makes sure her fingers are literally just inches from Jenn's pussy. Jenn feels the tighter grip but also feels Kate's fingers so close to her wetness. She braces herself with anticipation knowing her ass is about to feel the hard, stinging, slaps of Kate's hand.

Kate looks in the mirror and takes in the view. Once again, she loves what she sees... It looks fucking amazing! Kate's in her element and she gives no further warning as Jenn is securely in

179

place over her hip. Kate feels Jenn clench and brace herself as she expects a spanking, but instead Kate catches her by surprise and plunges her index and middle fingers deep into Jenn's pussy

Jenn is absolutely taken by complete surprise and reacts by pressing deeper into Kate's leg moaning with approval, "Aaaah… Mmmm. That feels AMAZING!

Kate plunges her two fingers farther into Jenn's wet pussy, as she holds her securely over her hip. She continues to give her sexy friend quite a finger fucking.

"Keep that ASS UP!" Kate commands as her two fingers penetrate Jenn's pussy.

She watches herself in the mirror holding Jenn over her hip and fingering her into oblivion. The image Kate sees of herself dominating Jenn makes her own pussy flood with wetness. Jenn is extremely turned on as she feels Kate's pretty fingers penetrating deep and exploring every inch of her. Her deep breaths and sexy moans validate exactly how she feels. Jenn doesn't hold back… She can't hold back, it feels amazing to her as she lets it all out. The kink room is now filled with the sounds of low music, in harmony with Jenn's heavy breathing, and sexy moans…

"Aaaahhh… MMMmmmm.. Oooooh."

"That's it, let it out, Jennifer! I want to

know exactly how this feels." Kate calls out as she continues to finger her.

Jenn's pussy is flooding with wetness as she replies with a deep breath, "Oh my God, aahhh... It feels so fucking good, Ma'am. I'm really close..."

Kate pauses for a second, then pulls her fingers out to prolong Jenn's orgasm. Jenn gasps as her pussy remains quivering and wanting more. Kate releases Jenn from her hip and helps to steady her back in the position of standing straight up. She then walks around her, until once again she stands face to face with her blindfolded friend.

Kate takes her fingers that have all of Jenn's sexy wetness on them and places in them in her mouth. She licks every inch of them, giving her a sample of how Jenn's pussy tastes.

"You taste so fucking good!" Kate tells her.

Jenn, still blindfolded, doesn't see Kate tasting her wetness but it's obvious as she can hear Kate sucking her fingers.

Kate then sticks her tongue out and once again engulfs Jenn lips with a passionate kiss. Jenn opens wider and lets her tongue explore Kate's mouth as she remains standing in the center of room.

"You are one sexy woman!" Jenn responds

with a deep, heated breath.

"I'm going to lick your pussy like an ice cream cone!" Kate tells her.

Jenn is crazy turned on hearing Kate talk dirty to her. She is doing all she can not to move and so desperately wants to rip off the blindfold and see her sexy friend doing all this to her.

"I want to see you, Ma'am... Please!" She asks Kate.

"Not yet, Jennifer... I've just begun... Tongue out!" Kate responds with her sexy voice.

Jenn listens and sticks her tongue out. Kate embraces it again into a hot, steamy kiss. Then, she reaches down and once again plunges her two fingers into Jenn's pussy.

Jenn is caught by surprise again. She screams out in pleasure, "Aaaaahhhhh..... Mmm-mmm."

Kate once again pulls her fingers out and this time places them in Jenn's mouth making sure she tastes herself.

"I want you to taste how delicious your pussy is!" Kate tells her.

Jenn still breathing heavy, listens and licks every bit of Kate's fingers as she whispers to her friend, "You are one sexy, kinky, fucker, Kate...

And I love it!"

Kate smirks and pulls her fingers out of Jenn's mouth and without any warning pulls her into her signature position and delivers a series of intense slaps across her bare ass! <SLAP, SLAP, SLAP, SLAP, SLAP>

Jenn immediately responds, "OOOOw... Ouch!"

Kate holds her in place right back over her hip and administers another flurry of hard, stinging hand slaps. <SLAP, SLAP, SLAP, SLAP>

Jenn squirms but to no avail as Kate firmly holds her in place.

"Tonight, I'm Ma'am or Miss... I'm not Kate.. Got it?" Kate scolds her.

Jenn quickly replies, "Yes Ma'am.... Sorry Ma'am."

Kate dishes out another five intense slaps. <SLAP, SLAP, SLAP, SLAP, SLAP>

Jenn's ass is now quickly colored red with Kate's hand prints. The intense slaps make her respond loudly, "OOOOww!... Sorry Ma'am... OOOhh!"

Kate again releases Jenn from over her hip. She proceeds to lift Jenn's dress completely over her head and totally off of her toned, curvaceous body. She temporarily guides her arms off the cable grips to remove Jenn's lace bra. She then puts Jenn's hand back on the grips and moves on and takes off her shoes. Jenn is now even more vulnerable as she's standing completely naked and still blindfolded in the center of the room.

Kate walks away and places the clothing on a table in the far end of the room. She then reaches into her toy bag in the closet and returns to the center of the room.

"Arms down... At your side!" She commands in her stern tone.

Jenn immediately listens and places both of her arms at her sides. As she stands there in the center of Kate's kink room, she knows that Kate is seeing her from every angle. Despite her insecurities, she loves this feeling of being vulnerable and embraces her kinky, exhibitionist side. She feels Kate tie both of her wrists together with rope. Once again she feels Kate guide her arms back up and over her head.

Kate securely ties them to the overhead cable grip and once again stands face to face in front of her. She now touches and fondles Jenn's perky tits as she lays another passionate kiss on her.

Their tongues connect as Jenn feels the tenderness and warmth of Kate's hands exploring her sun kissed tits. She loves the contrast of how hard Kate's hand felt a few seconds ago spanking her ass, to the way they feel now gently fondling her tits. She also loves the way Kate's tongue tastes in her mouth and the way her fingers felt in her pussy. Kate leaves her left hand touching and massaging Jenn's tits as her finger takes another unsuspecting plunge into Jenn's pussy.

Jenn responds with fire, "AAHHHHHH!"

Kate continues kissing her with passion as her hand and fingers are pleasuring her sexy friend. Jenn squirms and wiggles with elation but since her hands remain tied over her head, her movement is limited. The blindfold that's still in place over her eyes, causes her senses to just react to the way Kate feels and tastes.

Jenn lets her know, "I love it Ma'am... It feels so good!"

"Excuse me?" Kate sternly replies.

Jenn quickly reiterates, "It feels so FUCK-ING good!"

Kate walks and re-positions to the right side of Jenn's body as her two fingers stay deep in her pussy. Once again, she places her entire mouth over her ear, then she starts to talk dirty to her.

"Your pussy feels amazing, Jennifer! I love fingering this wet, juicy, pussy of yours. I love tasting your wetness on my fingers. I love reddening that amazing ass and seeing my hand prints on it."

Jenn's now panting, breathing heavy, and moaning with pleasure, "Mmmmm, I'm so turned on… You are driving me fucking crazy!"

Kate fingers her pussy harder and faster as Jenn calls out, "I'm close."

Once again, Kate pauses then removes her fingers to let Jenn's orgasm build even deeper inside of her. She walks away from Jenn and takes a moment to let her recover. Kate heads back into her toy bag as her mind continues to spawn more ideas.

Jenn remains tied and blindfolded in the center of the room, totally turned on and literally on the brink of an epic orgasm. Kate turns up the volume of the music as she walks back to her.

Of course Jenn doesn't know that Kate has several items in her hand. She has no idea where Kate is. The music fills her ears and the thick floor mats muffle all the background noise, so Jenn can't even hear the sound of Kate walking around her.

Kate looks at the reflection of her sexy friend tied in the middle of her kink room and again pauses to take in the view from every angle. Then, she glances at the doorway and gives a sexy smirk, placing her right index finger over her mouth. They are no longer alone as she makes the

The Academy Series (Orientation, Kick Off Dance, Play

"shush" gesture, indicating "be quite".

Her company is now here!

CHAPTER FIVE

◆ ◆ ◆

K ate's plan and kinky scenario continues to develop. She is no longer alone with Jenn tied and blindfolded in the center of her kink room. Jenn has no idea and totally oblivious to any of this. Her mind is just focused and wondering what Kate will do next. The blindfold has totally taken away her sense of sight. The music playing totally robs her sense of hearing any background noise. Her movement is greatly restricted with her arms tied over her head. The only thing Jenn can do is wait until Kate makes another move on her.

Kate looks thru the doorway and motions, giving the sign to come in. She quickly points to some of the stools and benches in her kink room.

It's obvious that her motion means sit, be completely quiet, and just watch.

"Now let's address your bad behavior, Jennifer!" She scolds and without wasting another second, she swings her reform strap and it connects loudly to Jenn's beautiful, bare ass. <CRACK!>

"OOOOww!" Jenn calls out as she feels the intense sting come out of nowhere and without a warning.

Kate delivers another two swats. <CRACK, SMACK>

Jenn twists and tucks her body inward as her ass sizzles. "OOOW... OUCH!"

She reacts and dances from leg to leg as her arms remained tied overhead. She has no idea that her ass is being viewed by anyone other than Kate. Kate approves with a signature smirk and reminds her sexy friend just how much she loves seeing her ass dance, "I love making that beautiful ass of yours bounce and clench, Jennifer!"

Kate reaches out and grabs Jenn's hips as she escorts her back in place.

"C'mon, stick it out... yep, right there..." Kate instructs her. She moves to Jenn's left side and with a firm grip places her hand around Jenn's left bicep to hold her in place. She swings the reform strap again and delivers another painful flurry.

<CRACK, CRACK>

"Yeoooow!" Jenn's voice resonates thru the room.

"Bad girls like you, will always get a good old fashion strapping from me!" Kate scolds. Once again Jenn continues twisting, tucking inwards, and clenching her ass cheeks in response to the strapping that Kate is administering.

<CRACK, CRACK, CRACK>

The blindfold covers most the tears from Jenn's eyes but a few manage to roll down her face. Kate becomes fully aware of this, as it confirms that Jenn is getting the release she desperately needed. With Jenn sobbing, Kate releases her grip and walks around to view Jenn's ass from every angle and especially right up close. She kneels down behind her and lets her tongue trace over the red stripes that her reform strap just created.

Jenn feels Kate's tongue on her ass and now responds in contrast with a sexy moan of approval. Kate immediately spins Jenn around as her hands tightly hold onto her hips. Her face is directly in front of Jenn's wet pussy and without prolonging it any longer, she buries her tongue deep inside, tasting all of her!

Jenn lets out a loud, sexy, pleasure filled moan, "Aaaahhhhh!"

Since the blindfold remains on, Jenn is caught totally off guard again. There is no way she can predict what Kate was, or is going to do. All she knows is that she's lost in the feeling of how amazing Kate's tongue feels in her pussy right now. Kate also takes the time and uses her full, plushy lips to gently kiss and suck Jenn's clit. Jenn is now squirming but in a way that is much different to the way she was squirming a few seconds ago.

Her mind is totally connected to everything that is her body is feeling. She gets even further turned on just thinking about how taboo this play date with Kate is. She's totally engulfed and aware how her emotions are like a ping-pong ball right now. Kate is alternating between giving her pleasure and giving her pain, and she's never experience anything like this in all her life.

Jenn is moaning up a storm as Kate's tongue is working wonders and exploring deep into her wet pussy and back out over her clit. She also gives Jenn's pussy some nice, soft kisses as she gently sucks and tastes every ounce of her wetness. Jenn's tears of pain have now changed to tears of ecstasy as she's experiencing all these various emotions.

Kate is crazy turned on as well from dominating her. She suddenly takes her fingers and plunges them underneath her sexy underwear to play with herself. She immediately lets out her own sexy moan that echoes thru the room. She starts to finger herself while she continues to go down on Jenn. Her adrenaline is on fire as her ex-hibitionist side is in full effect knowing eyes are watching.

Kate compliments, "God, your pussy tastes amazing!"

Jenn quickly responds through her deep moans, "Aaaah… You feel so good.. I fucking love it!"

Kate stands up and faces her. She places both of her hands on Jenn's pretty face and kisses her with everything she has. Jenn tastes herself on Kate's tongue and continues to breath deep, ex-pressing how incredibly turned on she is.

Kate motions and gives a signal with her hand as she continues to kiss Jenn. Just then an-other loud <CRACK> fills the room followed by Jenn's response, "Oooow!"

Kate continues to kiss her and hold her face in her hands as the sound of the reform strap con-nects another two times to Jenn's bouncing ass. <CRACK, CRACK>

Jenn can't help it as she clenches her ass, twists, and dances from leg to leg due to the sting of the strap. Her movement is pretty restricted with her arms tied overhead, in addition to Kate holding her tightly. She's so caught up in the moment and in the contrast of emotions that she's experiencing, that she doesn't even realize what's going on.

Then after a few moments it dawns on her. She realizes and asks herself…. Since Kate is kissing and holding me, who the fuck is strapping my ass?

Kate now snaps her fingers and points in the direction of Jenn's pussy. Jenn now experiences a total mind fuck. She feels Kate's tongue kiss her lips, then enter her mouth, but now at the same time she feels another tongue plunge deep into her pussy!

Her breathing is now as deep as it's ever been and she calls out, "I'm close Ma'am."

Kate snaps her fingers and suddenly everything stops leaving Jenn hanging on a thread and moaning, "Uuuuh."

Kate walks around her blindfolded and restrained friend and motions to the mysterious person to move away. She says nothing and gives Jenn a couple minutes to recoup as the music continues to block out the movement in the room.

She asks, "Are you enjoying this play date, Jennifer?"

Jenn responds immediately, "I'm in heaven… You're blowing my mind!"

"I'll take that as a YES then!" Kate responds back.

CHAPTER SIX

❖ ❖ ❖

Kate lets a few more minutes go by without doing or saying a thing. She walks over to her toy bag in the closet and again takes some items out. Jenn remains blindfolded and restrained totally naked in the center of the mirrored kink room. She's still trying to figure out who the mysterious stranger is that was spanking her and going down on her.

Jenn is unaware as Kate motions again. Suddenly a pair of lips touch Jenn's and penetrate her mouth. She immediately knows they are male as she can feel the short stubble of facial hair. Kate motions again and now Jenn feels another set of lips kissing and gently sucking her pussy. Her mind explodes as she also senses these lips belonging to another male. Just when Jenn doesn't think it can get any better she feels a mouth covering her entire right ear breathing heavy and gently kissing her earlobe and neck.

She lets out another moan in pure delight, "Mmmmmm.... Yes!"

Jenn is totally blown away as she now has no idea how many people are in the kink room. Furthermore, she has no idea who they are and only guesses from all she's feeling that it feels like three men along with Kate.

She then hears Kate call out from behind her, "You are so stunningly beautiful.. I think it's time to see yourself and take all this in!"

Her body starts to shake from the anticipation of it all. Kate then in a loud stern voice calls out, "Stop!" and sends a motion with her hand.

All action comes to a complete standstill as everyone moves away from Jenn. Kate once again stands to Jenn's left side and pulls her over her hip. Jenn feels herself getting pulled again. It's that same position that she knows all to well. She feels Kate's left arm wrap around her and underneath her stomach. She feels the familiar pull that forces her to arch her ass even more outward. Jenn is bracing herself as she anticipates another round of Kate's hand to once again take her from pleasure to pain. As she lays draped over Kate's curvy hip she lets out a sexy, "Mmmmmm!"

This was not a slap that she feels. Instead,

she feels Kate's finger plunge deep into her ass as she further moans. Kate is holding her in place and burying her pretty index finger deep inside.

Jenn moans, "Aaahhhh…Mmmm"

Kate coaches her, "Give me a deep breath, Jennifer."

Jenn listens and breathes in deep as she feels Kate's finger move in and out of her ass. Once again, she is forced to respond, "I'm so close!"

Kate calls out, "Now!"

Suddenly, like a choreographed danced team, everyone takes their position and goes to work on Jenn. Jenn feels a tongue plunge into her pussy. Then she feels another tongue plunge into her mouth as she's moaning. She then feels another mouth kiss her up and down her neck. A deep, sexy male voice then whispers into her ear, "Stick your beautiful ass out for Kate!"

Kate holds her in place over her hip and keeps her finger deep into Jenn's ass. She wiggles it a little, and instructs her, "Breath in… take a deep breath."

Jenn takes a deep breath as she feels another finger plunge into her pussy to accompany the tongue licking her clit. She feels Kate's finger in her ass and the other mystery finger in her pussy almost touching inside of her.

She responds, "Aaahhhh…"

Kate moves her finger almost out of Jenn's ass and then gives it one nice, long, deep plunge as she coaches her, "Cum for me, babe!"

Jenn wiggles and shakes….. Tongues, lips, and fingers are all over her body. She's now trembling in response to her approaching orgasm. She emits a beautiful and sexy moan, as tears stream down her face from underneath the blindfold. Kate gives the signal as a mystery man removes Jenn's blindfold.

Jenn slowly opens her eyes as they adjust to the lighting and the room. She looks to her right and into the mirror. She see's Kate fingering her ass. That image is insane looking and she now has it captured and embedded in her mind forever.

Then she looks down and sees a beautiful girl with a mask licking and fingering her pussy. Directly in front of her she sees a hot, muscular, stranger wearing an eye patch and a red bandanna kissing her lips. She looks to the side and catches a glimpse of another buff, masked man, squeezing her tits and kissing her neck.

She's feeling complete euphoria as tears are rolling down her face. She calls out, "I'm gonna… Aaaah…"

Kate keeps fingering her ass and replies

again, "Cum for me babe!"

Jenn trembles, moans, and fully lets go, "AHHHH!"

She lets out one last orgasmic scream as her entire body shakes in pleasure. Jenn climaxes and her body spasms into an orgasm. Kate smiles with approval and waits for Jenn to return back to earth. She gently removes her finger and motions for everyone else to stop as well. She walks over and removes the latex glove she was wearing and throws it in the garbage pail.

She then walks over and starts to untie her sexy friend. Jenn is overcome with emotions and just starts crying as she hugs Kate with every ounce of strength she has. She looks up into Kate's big green eyes, "That was the most intense, sexy, amazing, fucking experience I ever had!"

Kate kisses her cheek and gives her a towel, "Need a shower?"

Jenn replies, "God, yes.... Can I first say hi and thank everyone?"

Kate smiles and waves everyone to come close. Jenn wraps the towel around her as she takes it all in. She looks around and is in awe of how amazing the kink room looks with candles echoing in harmony with the soft lighting. Kate lowers the music so that introductions can properly be made.

Jenn now takes a moment to fully notice everyone's outfits. Her eyes immediately focus and start with Kate.

Kate looks absolutely insane wearing a sexy pirate outfit that has her red undies peaking thru a sheer black mini-skirt. Her bare legs lead down to a sexy pair of black boots. She has a black corset pulled tight around her torso as her blonde hair is tucked under a red & white bandanna.

"Fuck, you are one sexy woman!" Jenn compliments to her.

Kate then properly introduces all of her fellow pirate playmates. She pulls the buff mystery man close to Jenn, "This handsome pirate is Zachary… Zach.. He's my lieutenant in charge of the wenches." Everyone laughs at Kate's first introduction.

Zach removes his mask and the bandanna around his head, then extends his arms and gives Jenn a warm hug, "Nice to meet you.. You're stunning!"

"Damn, you're HOT! Nice to meet you Lieutenant Zach. You're voice and lips are still in my ear!" Jenn comments and chuckles.

The laughter continues at Jenn's sense of humor and Kate goes on.

"This sexy, tattooed, bad ass, is Eden... Zach's fiance. She's my first mate." Eden removes her mask and also says hello, giving Jenn a nice, warm hug.

Jenn looks at her, "You are stunningly beautiful Eden. Nice to meet you, love your tattoos... And oh, thank you for the tongue and finger action! It was fucking amazing!"

Eden laughs, "You're welcome... You're delicious and insanely beautiful yourself!" She then kisses Jenn on the cheek.

Jenn makes another comment, "Oh and Zach... You're a lucky fuck.. She's a keeper!"

Kate grabs the last mystery man, "This sexy fucker is Taylor. I'm sure you remember him.... He's the bad boy that I took behind the curtain at the fetish club in Springfield. Remember? I strapped his ass good! He's my hot commandeer and the one that helped me organize this."

"Oh yes, I remember that night and this sexy bad boy. Hello Taylor! Thank you for helping arrange this and for those sexy kisses. I'm still savoring the taste of your tongue!" Jenn jokes and continues to compliment all of them.

"You all look so amazing! I love the costumes, they are BAD ASS!"

"I honestly can't thank you guys enough. That was the best sexual experience that I ever had. This is one play date that I will never forget for the rest of my life!" Jenn smiles as she wipes the last few remaining tears from her eyes.

Kate sends a cute smile her way.

"Why don't you get cleaned up, babe. You can grab something out of my closet upstairs and come back down. We're not letting these costumes go to waste. That was only Round One! I have to make sure my fellow pirates are taken care of! You might want to watch or jump back in...."

"Both... see you in 15 minutes!" Jenn smirks at everyone.

CHAPTER SEVEN

◆ ◆ ◆

J enn heads upstairs and jumps in the shower. She cleans up in record time and goes thru Kate's closet as her creativity revs up. She also goes thru her bag to see if she can add anything extra to the mix.

Kate remains in the kink room with Taylor, Zach, and Eden. They are all back in character as Kate has them single file in a line. She's going to each one of them asking them a series of questions. She starts with Taylor, her commandeer. She wants to know why Zach and Eden are slacking off on their duties.

She turns to Zach and wants to know why Taylor orders haven't been followed. Of course, Zach gets right into the role play and explains that Taylor never informed him or Eden of their duties. That's why he failed to keep an accurate log report.

She turns and fires off a series of questions to Eden, who gives Kate a totally different response as Zach regarding Commandeer Taylor. Eden mentions that Taylor has been a great commandeer and that Lieutenant Zachary is spreading lies.

Just then, Jenn comes back to the kink room all cleaned up and rocking a make shift pirate outfit. She's killing it wearing a black blazer tied tight around her waist and hanging just long enough to cover her ass. She has her beautiful bare legs leading down to thigh high black boots. She tied a white bandanna around her head and added some dark eyeliner and makeup to complete the look.

Kate looks in her direction and gives her the approval, "Captain Jennifer, nice of you to join us.... front and center." Jenn listens and stands at attention in the center of the room.

Kate grabs Taylor and turns to the women, "Tie him to that chair and blindfold him!"

Jenn, and Eden move quickly to blindfold Taylor and secure him to a chair at the far end of the room. Kate now focuses her attention on Zachary.

"Lieutenant Zachary, you are under arrest

and subject to our punishment. If you agree to co-operate you will be properly rewarded at the end. Do you freely accept your punishment?" Kate asks him.

Zachary replies, "Yes Ma'am, I accept."

"Very well!" Kate responds to him as she quickly moves behind him and grabs hold of both arms.

"Eden, since Zachary tried to get you in trouble, I give you permission to go into my closet and select any implement you would like to use on him." Kate further instructs.

The dark haired, bad ass, pirate goes into Kate's closets and returns with a black riding crop.

Eden looks at Kate and raises the crop, "This is my selection, Ma'am."

Kate nods her head in a yes motion and tightens her grip holding onto Zach's arms. She gives Jenn a familiar look, "Captain Jenn, you know what to do!"

Jenn doesn't hesitate and jumps right into the scene as she approaches Zach. Her adrenaline is revving up as she always enjoys this part of a disciplining. She has that stern, no nonsense, look on her face as she stands face to face with him. Then she does her thing! With no hesitation what-soever, she grabs his black pirate pants and aggres-sively yanks them down to his ankles.

She returns to staring face to face with him as she gets more into her part. Jenn's eyes have that look in them as she puts both hands on the waistband of his underwear and pauses for moment.

"You are in for a serious disciplining, Lieutenant Zachary!" She warns him.

Once again, she gives an aggressive pull and escorts his underwear down to his ankles. Jenn and Eden both smile as they get a great view of Zachary's dick, complete with a full hard on. Eden reaches down with her right hand and grabs his balls with a firm grip.

She looks right into his eyes, "This is quite beautiful, Zachary!"

Kate and Jenn smile at each other as they look around the kink room and catch the reflections of everyone thoroughly enjoying this role play. Even Taylor is still smiling from hearing the dialogue, as he's blindfolded and tied in the far corner of the room.

"Name your position, Eden." Kate instructs her.

Eden responds, "Both of you take an arm and spin him ass out!"

Jenn grabs Zachary's left arm as Kate grabs his right. They spin him around with his tight, muscular ass facing Eden. She smirks, raises the crop and delivers! <SMACK>

Zach is rock hard as Kate and Jenn hold him in place. They make sure to get a nice view of his thick dick, as well as his tight, round, ass. They hold onto him tighter as Eden delivers five in a row with the crop. <SMACK, SMACK, SMACK, CRACK, CRACK>

Zach tucks his body inward, clenches his ass, and grimaces, "Uuuuuuuh."

Jenn reaches down with her left hand and cups Zachary's balls. She gives them a firm squeeze and continues to thrive in her character.

"Arch that ass out, Zachary!" Jenn commands him.

Kate smiles with approval as she sends a cute smirk to Jenn. Inside she glows and thinks herself…. Damn, I sure taught her well.

Eden raises her right arm and administers another five with the crop. <CRACK, SMACK, CRACK, CRACK, SMACK>

Kate reaches down and places her hand next to Jenn's. Jenn conveniently slides her hand over to make room for Kate to cop a feel. Kate now firmly grabs his balls and commands… "You better keep that ass out, Zachary!"

<SMACK, CRACK, SMACK> Eden delivers three more with the crop. Zach continues to clench his ass tight as the red marks take effect. Eden flashes her stern, bad ass, bitch look to Jenn and Kate. Time for him to really dance! She delivers the crop with serious intensity! <SMACK> Zach now raises his right leg off the ground, "OOW!" as Jenn and Kate tightly hold his arms. Eden doesn't wait and delivers two more serious spanks with the riding crop. <SMACK, CRACK>

Zach immediately raises his left leg off the ground and then his right leg again. He's definitely dancing from leg to leg as his voice expresses what his ass is feeling. Eden's shoots the women her devilish grin, as she loves seeing him dance and shuffle like this from the sting of the crop.

She turns to Kate and says, "Thank you Ma'am!"

Kate and Jenn release Zachary and he immediately grabs his ass to soothe it. The impact of the crop has painted some nice red marks on his muscular ass cheeks. His dick is now at an epic proportion and pointed straight up north. Kate turns to Jenn with her cute, devilish smirk.

"How do you want him?" She asks her.

Jenn quickly responds, "Over my knee with my wooden spoon!"

Jenn goes into her bag of tricks and pulls out a nice, old fashion, wooden spoon. She then pulls a chair into the middle of the floor as Kate marches him over to her.

Zachary stands at Jenn's side as his dick continues to point straight up. She grabs his left arm and pulls him over her sexy lap. His huge cock presses right into her bare leg as her hands grab his ass and position him right where she wants him. Jenn raises her wooden spoon and delivers a serious spanking. <CRACK, SMACK, SMACK, CRACK, SMACK>

Zach immediately starts to squirm and reaches back with his right arm. Jenn quickly grabs onto it and pins it behind his back. She has no problem holding his arm there with force as she demonstrates her experience in giving a serious spanking. It's very clear that she is a stern, no nonsense disciplinarian when she needs to be.

She smirks, "Nice try, Lieutenant!"

Once again she raises the wooden spoon and continues to add more redness to his tight ass.

<SMACK, SMACK, SMACK, CRACK>

Zachary really responds to Jenn's spanking, "OOOooooow.... Uuuhhh.... Ooow."

Jenn scolds, "I'm not done with you yet… I'll teach you a lesson about telling lies!"
<SMACK, SMACK, SMACK, SMACK, CRACK, CRACK>

Jenn finishes administering the wooden spoon spanking. Zachary's ass now has bright, red, spoon prints to compliment the crop marks. Once again, Jenn feels herself getting extremely wet. She loved having his hard cock press into her leg and watching his ass clench tight as she was administering his spanking. Needless to say, this spanking got her firing on all cylinders as her adrenaline is revved up to full force.

She pulls him up and looks at Kate, "Done Ma'am!"

Kate resumes her character as she walks over to Zachary.

"You took your punishment well Lieutenant Zachary. I want you to whisper in my ear on what you would like your reward to be." Kate directs him.

Zach does so as Kate shoots the girls a smirk and goes to tell them about Zach's fantasy. She whispers in Jenn's ear and then in Eden's ear. Jenn shoots Eden a cute smile confirming that she likes what she just heard from Kate. She then walks over to Zachary and is completely ready to fill this part of his fantasy.

She kneels down at his feet, cups his balls tightly with her left hand, and grabs onto his thick dick with her right hand. Jenn is more than happy as she smiles at this handsome hunk of a man. She slowly takes all of his cock in her pretty mouth, immediately making Zach's breathing heavy and deep. She wraps her full lips tightly around the shaft of his dick, and starts sucking it like a lollipop. Zachary's low voice is giving her all the feedback she needs to hear. He responds with some sexy moans all his own.

"Ahhhh… mmm… fuck yeah!"

Jenn continues to lick right up to the tip of his dick and then all the way down to his balls. Her left hand is still fondling and squeezing his balls as her right hand is stroking him. Her blow job is amazing and gives him a different variation of something he commonly gets from Eden, his fiance.

Her mouth is taking every inch of him in, as she alternates between sucking his dick and licking the tip of it. She keeps a firm hold of it as she continues to run her tongue all the way down the shaft and onto his balls.

Zachary is in heaven and absolutely loving Jenn's blowjob. His breathing becomes heavier and his sexy moans are really turning Jenn on as well. Eden has a smile on her face from ear to ear confirming that she loves watching her man with another woman. Especially a hot, older, sexy, woman like Jenn.

Zach's moans become louder and nicely fill the kink room. Kate senses that he is getting close to climaxing. She continues to watch his reactions as Jenn delivers an epic blowjob.

Kate waits a few more seconds and then calls out, "Now Eden."

Eden now walks over, lowers her panties, and bends over the stool that Jenn was sitting on. Jenn stops blowing him, allowing Zach to complete his fantasy. He's turned on to the max and doesn't waste any time as he grabs Eden's hips and mounts her with force.

Zach sticks his dick deep into her pussy as she lets out a moan. He fucks her hard and with forceful thrusts, using everything he's got. It's her turn to scream now but in a different way. Not only does he love hearing her moan, he also knows from experience exactly how she likes it! Eden begins to moan as Zach pounds her and watches her cute ass bounce from his deep thrusts.

Kate moves in front of Eden and begins to kiss her lips to add to this fantasy. This gives Eden an additional sensation as her man is fucking the daylights out of her. Kate then reaches down and takes her perky tits into her hands. Eden loves feeling the multiple sensations of Zach fucking her, while Kate is kissing and feeling her. Her mouth opens wide and swallows Kate tongue as she moans with pleasure.

Jenn follows the plan to fulfill Zach's fantasy as she snaps on a latex glove and dips her right index finger into Vaseline. She positions herself slightly off to Zach's left side as he's fucking Eden. Jenn is watching and waiting for just the right time to take Zach over the edge.

Zach was well aware that his fantasy would also be one that his fiance would truly enjoy. He continues to fuck Eden with serious intensity, as his moans let everyone know he isn't far away. Jenn observes closely, watching Zach's reactions, as she prepares for his finale.

Needless to say, she was beyond pleased when Kate told her that he specifically wanted her to do this. It's something that she absolutely loves doing as her adrenaline is spiked to max.

She waits another few seconds, observing, and knows that now is the time to deliver. She casts a pretty little smirk, then inserts her index finger deep into his ass. Zach tightens and clenches his ass around her finger in response. Jenn feels him tighten and further pushes it deeper in. Then, she holds it firmly in place. Her smile says it all as she absolutely loves doing this, especially since her vanilla husband doesn't let her finger anywhere near his ass.

Jenn's pussy is now soaking, wet again with desire as her finger is buried deep in Zach's tight, muscular ass. Zach continues to fuck Eden hard and gives her several really intense thrusts. This sends him over the edge as he climaxes and lets out a sexy moan, "Aaaaaah!"

Kate smirks at Jenn as she pauses from kissing Eden. Her smiles speaks volumes as she knows Jenn is enjoying this as well. Jenn smiles back at her and keeps her finger deep into Zach's ass until she's sure his orgasm is completely over. Once it's clear that he's finished, she removes her finger and discards the latex glove she put on.

Zach is totally spent as he pulls out of Eden. He looks at Kate and moves his lips, making just a little bit of sound with a whisper, "Thank you!"

Kate smiles back at him and at Jenn, "Another happy camper!"

Kate then turns her attention back to Eden as she continues to kiss her. Eden is loving Kate's lips and her tongue. She is moaning and breathing heavy as she kisses Kate with intense passion. She reaches down and places her hand under Kate's skirt. She starts rubbing Kate's pussy and let's her fingers slide inside of her panties.

Kate takes a deeper breath as she feels Eden's fingers enter her pussy. She continues to kiss her as Eden now works her fingers in small circles. Kate is loving it as she expresses thru her sexy looks and passionate moans. She pauses for moment and looks directly into Eden's eyes.

"Round Three is all yours. What's your fantasy, Hun?" She asks her.

CHAPTER EIGHT

❖ ❖ ❖

Eden's lost in the moment. Her pussy is throbbing from just having her fiance fuck her with intensity until he climaxed. At the same time, she had Kate's full, beautiful lips and sexy tongue kissing her. Plus, now her fingers just started exploring Kate's pussy and she's enjoying every second of doing that as well. She pauses for a moment to focus her attention on answering Kate's question. She knows it's her turn now. What fantasy does she want to play out right now in the kink room with 4 very attractive, very kinky people? Decisions, decisions.....

Eden looks at everyone in the room with a cute, devilish grin. She smiles at her man Zach, then shoots Kate a sexy look. She eyes Jenn up and down, and then focuses her eyes on Taylor. She contemplates her move as several kinky thoughts revolve in her mind. She makes her decision and then whispers it into Kate's ear.

Kate goes to the back of the room and unties Taylor. She whispers directly in his ear as she also takes his blindfold off. He flashes her his "hell yeah", bad boy, smile and walks toward Eden. His big, brown, eyes gaze with intensity on the dark haired beauty.

Kate then commands Zachary to sit on the chair Taylor just occupied and watch. Eden's eyes light up as Taylor, with all his hotness, approaches her. She smiles at him and starts to give him a tasteful striptease. One by one, she teases and takes off the remaining pieces of clothing she still has on.

Taylor, as well as, everyone else is more than delighted to watch Eden's strip show. Over time and to the rhythm of the music, her pirate outfit accumulates on the floor. Eden finishes her sexy striptease and stands totally naked in the middle of the kink room. She slowly turns in a complete circle giving everyone a full view of her stunning body. She manages to steal a few glances at herself, reflecting in the mirrors with the candles and soft lighting creating a favorable glow.

There is no doubt that she loves to embrace this exhibitionist side of her kink. Kate now whispers in Jenn's ear as Taylor takes Eden's hand and leads her to the large padded massage table. He lays on flat on his back and Eden wastes no time in getting into her position. She's ready to receive and totally fulfill her fantasy. She's maneuvers herself into a sixty-nine position with her legs straddling his face.

Zachary looks on and approves with a huge smile on his face. He loves this sexy side of her, and is in awe of the way his soon to be wife looks right now. Eden slowly starts gyrating her hips, once in while letting her body gently touch Taylor's face. His tongue fully extends as he grabs onto her cute ass with both his hands. With every little movement she makes, his tongue licks her clit and also quickly dips into her pussy.

Eden's moans fill the room as Zachary looks on and smiles from ear to ear. He can't help but just take in the view and enjoy how beautiful, sexy and happy she looks right now in this moment. He sees every bit of her womanly sexiness come out as she's laying over Taylor's face and getting her pussy licked.

It's a view that many men will never experience, understand, or appreciate unless they are open and comfortable enough to watch their significant other with another person. Zach and Eden both understand and embrace this. They use it like a tool, like a hammer and nails, to further build and strengthen their relationship.

Eden looks over and sends Zach a cute

smile. She then reaches down and lowers Taylor's pirate pants. She places his hard dick into her mouth and starts going to town on it. Taylor begins showing his appreciation by sending some sexy sounds and moans into the atmosphere.

Jenn follows thru with Eden's requests as she walks over with her wooden spoon in hand. She watches closely as the sexy girl continues her sixty-nine session with Taylor. Jenn waits for the right moment, raises her spoon, and gives Eden's right ass cheek a little swat. <crack> It's just enough to create the effect that Eden asked for as she lets out a nice sounding, "Mmmmm!"

Kate's ready for her part in Eden's fantasy as she walks over to Eden's left side carrying the riding crop. She watches Eden's sexy ass bounce over Taylor's face as her pussy feels the delight of his tongue. Kate waits for the right moment, then raises the crop and delivers a swat right across Eden's left ass cheek. <smack> Eden moans louder in approval, as her fantasy starts to really come to life.

She bounces and gyrates more intensely on Taylor's face as she lets out another moan, "Mmmmm!" She continues sucking his rock hard dick as she looks over and sends a sexy look with her eyes to her soon to be husband, Zach.

Zach loves watching her and smiles back, then whispers, "You're so fucking hot! I love you!"

Robin Fairchild

Eden now concentrates on herself and wants to fully appreciate and feel every sensation that's part of her fantasy. In order to do this, she needs to connect her mind to her body. She takes a break from sucking Taylor's dick to just get lost in the feeling of his tongue. She takes a moment to focus on how amazing her pussy feels right now. She closes her eyes and is ready to add another sensation to the mix.

She continues her slow, sexy grinds on him and calls out, "Spank my ass, Jenn!" Jenn does so with delight and delivers four swats with her wooden spoon using just the right amount of force to add to Eden's pleasure. <smack, smack, crack, smack>

Eden loves the contrast of Taylor's soft, gentle licks on her pussy combined with Jenn's stinging swats of the wooden spoon applied to her ass.

She moans in pleasure as she continues her slow grinds. She takes a deep breath and then calls out, "Spank me, Kate!"

Kate follows thru with four swats of the crop, again using just enough force to create the effect Eden asked for. <crack, smack, crack, crack>

Eden now calls out, "Lick my pussy faster Taylor… I'm so close!"

Taylor follows thru and increases the speed of his tongue all over her clit and deep into her pussy. Jenn and Kate alternate giving one spank at a time to Eden. Jenn delivers her spoon. <smack> Kate delivers her crop. <smack>

Taylor continues to vigorously eat her out and within a minute, she moans, "I'm Cumming!"

Eden stays pressed down on Taylor's face as Jenn and Kate deliver a few last swats together on each ass cheek. <crack, smack, crack, smack>

Eden orgasms and lets out a moan that is filled with total pleasure. Her body shakes in a euphoric pattern as the smile on her face confirms that her fantasy just came true. She takes a moment to bask in the feeling and then makes her way off the padded table. She turns to Kate and Jenn, and approaches them with open arms. She embraces them both in a tender hug and says thank you. She looks at Taylor and gives him a sexy kiss letting her tongue show her gratitude.

She then walks back to her fiance Zach with a huge smile, "I love you baby, that was fucking insane!"

Jenn looks at Kate this time, "Yep, another happy camper!"

Taylor laughs along with them and pulls his pants back up as he gets off the table. Kate turns and looks at him, "Where you think you're going sexy? You're next!"

Taylor looks back at her, with his confident, bad boy smirk. "It's your turn now, babe... Let me be last!" He tells her.

Jenn smiles at Kate, "Round Four is yours Kate. Who do you want to tell your fantasy to?"

CHAPTER NINE

◆ ◆ ◆

Kate looks at Taylor then walks over and whispers in his ear. He listens intently as her fantasy fills his head. He takes a moment as he's lost in thought and then looks back at her.

"I think we can actually combine yours and mine." He whispers back into Kate's ear.

Kate chuckles, "Perfect, then I'll start with mine and we'll add yours in!"

Kate slowly begins her version of a striptease. She moves her hips seductively to the music as all eyes gaze upon her. Piece by piece she removes her pirate outfit and everyone's eyes light up as more of her body gets revealed. Plain and simple, her body is insane looking, as the last few pieces of clothing are shed. Kate's now standing right there in front of everyone, completely naked in the middle of her kink room. She gives Jenn a sexy look, then walks over to her, and whispers the fantasy to her.

"God yes, I love it!" Jenn responds.

Jenn starts to engage her role in Kate's fantasy as she now also begins to remove her own clothing. Everyone's eyes get another treat as Jenn's striptease goes down. It doesn't take Jenn long to be completely naked and standing with Kate in the middle of the room. She then gives Kate a cute little kiss as she takes her hand and walks her over to the large padded massage table.

Jenn gets on the table and lays on flat her back, "Come on, babe."

Kate gives that trademark smirk of hers and joins Jenn on the table. She straddles herself over Jenn's face as the on lookers smile. Jenn immediately grabs onto Kate's amazing ass and forcefully spreads her cheeks apart. Kate breathes in deeply and presses her body further into Jenn's face. Jenn was more than happy to honor this fantasy as she immediately begins kissing, licking, and rimming Kate's beautiful, heart shaped ass.

Eden now takes a seat on Zachary's lap as together the couple enjoys experiencing the voyeuristic side of their kinky lifestyle. Taylor positions himself in front of the table and starts kissing Kate passionately as she wiggles her ass all over Jenn's tongue.

Jenn loves rimming her. She varies her approach with her tongue and gives Kate some nice, slow, gentle licks, followed by a few quick plunges, and even some cute little bites to her ass cheeks.

Kate is moaning in delight as her hips seductively gyrate and her ass tightens and clenches. She's so turned on and now lets out a sexy, "Mmmmm!"

Jenn loves hearing these sexy, pleasure induced sounds coming from Kate's mouth. She keeps her eyes fully open as she loves the view of Kate's perfect ass clenching and wiggling all over her face. She grabs Kate's ass even tighter and digs her finger nails into each cheek. She wants to return the favor and give Kate the contrast of pleasure and pain. This quick, little intense pinch of pain shocks Kate as her eyes light up with approval.

"Mmmmm… ouch…. mmm." Echoes from her mouth.

Kate's gyrations become a bit faster as Jenn now lets her tongue travel all around Kate's pussy. She starts slowly sucking her clit as her tongue takes frequent plunges deep into Kate's wetness.

Jenn is tasting all of her. She's returning the

favor and devouring every ounce of Kate's pussy with complete pleasure. She absolutely loves the way Kate is tasting on her tongue. In response, her pussy becomes saturated with wetness as well.

"Come on, babe... Wiggle that ass for me!" Jenn tells her.

Kate listens and pushes herself deeper onto Jenn's face as she clenches her ass tight with slow gyrations. She feels Jenn's tongue hitting every part of her ass, then traveling to her clit, and then exploring deep into her pussy.

Taylor lowers his pants and starts stroking himself. He's totally rock hard watching these two beautiful, sexy, women go at it on top of the padded table. The smiles on Eden and Zach's faces confirm they are enjoying seeing the Kate and Jenn show as well.

Kate continues to gyrate and expresses everything she's feeling by filling the room with her sexy moans. She's been primed the entire day. It started from early afternoon when her and Jenn began talking in the park, to the entire night at the student kick-off dance, and continued right thru fingering herself on the drive home, as she was thinking about this play date.

So right now everything is coming to a climax as she's lost in the feeling of complete elation. It doesn't take her long as her breathing is getting deeper and deeper for her voice to call out, "Mmmmm, I'm close…."

Jenn stops and lets Kate get into the right position in order to continue the fantasy. Kate maneuvers onto all fours, doggy style on the table. Her body looks incredible as she shifts her weight backwards. Zach and Eden's eyes are glued to her insane ass. This position makes it look even sexier, if that's possible, and it makes her curvy hips look even more beautiful.

She signals to Jenn who maneuvers into the same exact position beside her. Kate looks over her shoulder at Taylor and gives him a steamy look that's just killer, lighting up his soul.

"Come aboard you sexy fucker!" She tells him.

Taylor slips on a condom, grabs her beautiful hips, and immediately thrusts his hard dick deep into her pussy. She turns to Jenn and starts kissing her with fiery passion. Taylor goes at it hard making Kate moan loudly with every thrust. He keeps a nice tight grip on her hips as he rocks his muscular body back and forth deep into her. He's extremely turned on and sporting one massive hard on.

Kate is loving the way he's fucking her as she feels every inch of his manhood deep inside. Her tongue is locked onto Jenn as more of her senses come alive. She loves kissing her and tasting her tongue just as much as being fucked hard by Taylor.

Her sexy moans confirm it all. "Mmmmm… Aahhhhh… I'm getting close." She lets them both know.

Taylor pauses to tease Kate and add to her build up. He pulls his dick out of her pussy and grabs onto Jenn's hips. With the same intense force, his dick enters Jenn's soaking wet pussy. He repeats the same hard thrusts over and over as Jenn's moans with pure satisfaction.

Taylor loves fucking… not to mention, he's amazing at it! He has no problem fucking both of them into oblivion as now his energy is focused on Jenn. He pushes deep into her warm pussy as she feels him further penetrate her. Other than her husband, she hasn't fucked another guy or had her pussy feel like this for at least 15 years. No one, including the man she married, has turned her on the way she's turned on tonight.

Her breathing is heavy and labored but yet she still continues to kiss Kate with so much intensity. Jenn's beautiful moans now echo throughout the room adding to the visual as Zach and Eden continue to feast their eyes on this sexy scene.

Taylor teases Jenn and adds to her build up

also, as he pulls his dick out of her. He shoots that "sexy as fuck" look back over at Kate. He then grabs her and rolls her over onto her back. His muscular arms lift her legs until they are resting comfortably over his shoulders. His hands reach down, grab her ass, and spread her cheeks apart further opening her pussy. He quickly enters and penetrates deeply into her again.

Kate's pleasure filled voice expresses exactly how she feels, "Mmmmmm... Fuck, this feels amazing! Fuck me.. Harder.. Harder, babe!"

Jenn leans over and kisses Kate as her mouth opens wide to receive it. She loves the way Jenn's soft tongue feels in her mouth, while Taylor's hard thrust penetrate deep into her pussy. The texture, the passion, the taste, the sounds are driving her crazy as she approaches her climax.

Taylor continues to fuck her hard as her sexy moans fill everyone's ear. He senses that she may be getting really close. Once again, he teases the fuck out of her, but he knows in the end this will give her an insane orgasm. It takes all the strength he has to pull his dick out of Kate's warm pussy, but he does it, knowing the pay off will be worth it.

This time he grabs Jenn and rolls her over onto her stomach. He presses his hand firmly into the small of her back. Her body looks stunning and she's lying face down on the table. Her ass looks absolutely delicious in this position as Taylor grabs a hold of it. He pulls her cheeks apart with a bit of roughness and pushes his huge dick right back into her pussy.

Jenn gasps and responds with pleasure, "Aahhhhh... Yes, Mmmmm!"

Taylor listens to her moans and continues to fuck her with his bad boy, rough play, style. He is totally turned on and rocking Jenn's world. He shows her all that she's been missing and most likely has ruined her for life. Jenn is feeling all of him and she's loves having every inch of his dick deep inside her.

Kate maneuvers herself in the same position and lays down next to her. Once again, she delivers more passionate kisses to her, making Jenn's senses fully aroused with pleasure. Jenn's moans are undeniable. She's experiencing heaven as her body and mind are turned on more than she can ever remember.

Unable to hold it back any longer, she lets go, "AAAhhhh!"

Kate continues to bury her tongue deep into her mouth as she feels her sexy friend shake with another phenomenal orgasm. She continues to kiss and hold Jenn tight until every bit of her climax is over. Jenn's face streaming with joyous tears says it all. She looks deep into Kate's eyes expressing complete gratitude for this play date. Kate takes in this genuine "thank you" look, gives her one last kiss, and flashes her a sexy smile.

Taylor makes sure Jenn is completely done with her orgasm and then he pulls himself out her. He wastes no time as he calls back to Kate.

"Let's go, back to doggy style, babe!"

Kate goes back into her favorite position and once again she feels Taylor's dick penetrate her pussy. Her wetness is at an all time high as he's fucking her with reckless abandon. Taylor delivers a flurry of thrusts harder and harder until he can't hold it in any longer. His moans let everyone on planet earth know he's cumming.

Kate tightens her pussy around his cock, making the sensation even better for him. This rocks Taylor's world as his grip tightens around her hips. His dick pulses as his hot sperm quickly fills the condom. He might never be the same either after experiencing this play date. His body along with his mind have been blown into an epic climax. Kate makes sure Taylor's orgasm is complete and then turns over onto her back. She looks over to Zach and Eden with a kinky smirk. With a motion of her finger, she signals for Eden to come over.

Eden approaches with a huge smile as Kate rubs herself and sends a sexy look downward to her own pussy. Eden is all over it!

She immediately puts her tongue on the inside of Kate's legs and starts to lick upward. The sexy pirate grabs onto her ass cheeks and quickly navigates her tongue straight toward Kate's pussy. She's all in as her tongue licks around Kate's clit, frequently plunging into her pussy. The beautiful sounds coming from Kate's mouth are a quick approval of the way Eden's tongue is pleasuring her. Jenn now maneuvers herself off the table, stands up, and leans right back over it. She places her lips on Kate's as they embrace in an upside down kiss.

Kate is now feeling more turned on then ever. Eden is going down on her as Jenn's lips feel even more tantalizing kissing her in this position. Her hands reach up and grab onto Jenn's neck as they continue their sexy kiss, Taylor now signals for Zach to come over to Kate's left side as he walks over to her right. He starts kissing and fondling Kate's right breast as Zach follows his lead and focuses on her left.

Both men fondle, kiss, and gently suck each of Kate's perky tits using their own individual style. Taylor takes his tongue and slowly flattens it out completely covering all of Kate's strawberry nipple with each lick. Zach enjoys alternating between gently sucking and flicking his tongue on her nipple.

Kate's in a totally euphoric state as her

senses experience Jenn's soft lips and warm tongue in her mouth, while Taylor and Zach's tongue are licking her tits, and Eden's tongue is totally working her pussy over. Jenn decides to add even more intensity to the scene as she directs Taylor to switch places with her. His lips now give Kate a new texture in the same upside kiss position, as Jenn's tongue gives her a new variation teasing her breast.

Kate is loving it as her deep sexy breathing intensifies. Everyone is playing their part perfectly to create a world class finale for the sexy woman that arranged this kinky play date. They all continue to give Kate pleasure beyond description as each one of them uses their lips, tongue, fingers and special skills to further enhance all she's feeling. Jenn continues to softly kiss and suck on Kate's right breast as she directs and makes another change. She points to Zach and Taylor who follow her direction and switch places. This simple adjustment allows Kate to experience new sets of lips on different places on her body.

Kate appreciates the variations and responds, "Mmmmmm...yes....mmmm."

Zach now embraces Kate in an upside kiss as Taylor's mouth and tongue attend to her left breast. Jenn lets her fingers wander down to Kate's pussy as her lips and tongue stay focused on her right breast. Eden adjusts her tongue to concentrate on Kate's clit as she makes way and allows Jenn's fingers to explore Kate's pussy. Kate feels this new sensation and reacts favorably, "Aahhhh!"

Jenn knows that Kate is close to an orgasm as she takes her two fingers and buries them deeper into her pussy. Eden now makes her tongue flick in a rapid motion on Kate's clit as Jenn's fingers deeply arouse her pussy.

Kate moans, "Mmmmmm... mmmmm... I'm so close..."

Eden takes notices and is ready to complete Kate's fantasy and send her thru the roof with pure delight. She licks her right, index finger and then inserts it deep into Kate's sexy ass while she keeps her tongue licking and gently sucking her clit. Kate clenches her ass as she feels Eden's finger enter it.

She instantly reacts, "AAAhhh... Yes, Yes!" Jenn's finger travels deeper into her pussy, then she holds it there and coaches her sexy friend, "Breathe deep, babe... nice and deep!"

Kate takes a deep breath and allows her mind to really concentrate on the pleasure of everything she's feeling. She feels Zach kissing her lips and Taylor kissing her breast. She then focuses on Eden holding her finger deep into her ass as her tongue is licking and gently sucking her clit. She then connects her mind to Jenn's pretty fingers deep into her pussy while her sexy voice is whispering in her ear, "C'mon babe, deep breath....that's it... C'mon..."

Kate's sexy moan completes it, "AAAAAA-AAAAAHHhhhhhhhh!"

Her entire body rapidly trembles and spasms as she releases into an epic orgasm. This climax was building all day and she now experiences the release she desperately needed. Her mind was totally engaged and connected to her body as she created this amazing play date with some very sexy and kinky friends.

She takes a moment to come back down from heaven as everyone waits to make sure she is completely done with her release. Kate recovers as she looks at everyone and expresses her gratitude.

"Oh My God!! Thank you, Thank you, Thank you... That was insane! Holy Fuck..... You blew my mind!"

It's 2:30am Saturday morning and the play date comes to an end. Everyone changes back into comfortable clothing as they pack their pirate outfits and the accessories in their gym bags. One by one they compliment and thank each other as they say their goodbyes with loving hugs. Jenn remains as Kate locks the front door behind them and walks into her kitchen.

She lets out a deep breath, "PHHHeeeew!" That was FUCKING AMAZING!" She then extends an offer for Jenn to sleep over, "Hey babe, stay tonight...Take the guest room. I'm getting in the shower and then lets meet back down here. I plan on diving into a huge bowl of ice cream!"

Jenn wastes no time, "I know it's not vanilla... right?"

They both laugh and hug each other tight as Jenn accepts her offer.

"The Academy" series continues with book 4 of the story "The Proposition".

Printed in Great Britain
by Amazon